The Miss

Lou Elliott Mystery Adventure Series: Book 2

By

George Chedzoy

LOU ELLIOTT MYSTERY ADVENTURES:

1. Smugglers at Whistling Sands
2. The Missing Treasure
3. Something Strange in the Cellar
4. Trouble at Chumley Towers

To:

My mother Judy and my late father, Michael

The Missing Treasure
Lou Elliott Mystery Adventure Series Book 2

First published by George Chedzoy, 2013 in eBook format
First edition in paperback, 2016
This book: First edition, first print

CONTENTS

CHAPTER ONE

An exciting plan

THERE was only one week left of the summer holidays. Where did the time go? Jack had mixed feelings about returning to school. He couldn't wait to tell his schoolmates about their brush with smugglers during a family break on the North Wales coast. But he simply wasn't ready for the holidays to end just yet.

Things hadn't been quite so exciting since he and his brother David and sister Emily had returned home with their mum and dad after two weeks at Abersoch. While there, they had met a girl called Lou Elliott, aged 12 – the same as Jack – and with her had fallen into an amazing adventure.

That already seemed ages ago now. Jack gazed out of the window of their home in Malpas, a cheerful little village in Cheshire, and felt a touch despondent. Life was bound to feel a tad dull after all they had been through together. At least he would surely have the best summer holiday story to share with the others back at the Bishop Heber School.

If his schoolmates didn't believe that the four of them had stumbled upon the activities of smugglers, well he had sure proof – the newspaper and magazine articles written about it. That was down to Lou's dad, who worked as a journalist. He had sold their story around the world.

Jack had cut out all the articles and stuck them carefully in a scrapbook, interspersed with photographs he and the others had taken. The scrapbook lay in front of him on the coffee table. He picked it up and glanced at a picture of Lou. He wondered what she was up to at that moment.

She would most likely be back home in rural Shropshire. Lou was an only child and spent most of her time on her own, but she had loved becoming friends with them.

Jack yearned for the four of them to be back at Abersoch together – smugglers or no smugglers. At least Lou's parents weren't now going to sell off their seaside holiday cottage and, with any luck, they might see her at half-term. That wasn't until October of course, which seemed ages away.

If only they could all meet again before school started, but Jack couldn't see it happening. He sat back down on the sofa and flicked absentmindedly through the scrap-book. David sat the other end, his freckled face hidden behind an old, leather-bound book with gilt-edged pages. Only a mop of untidy, tousled brown hair could be seen protruding over the top. He looked, in fact, very similar to his elder brother although Jack's hair had turned fairer in the summer sunshine. David was not so stocky and strong as Jack but from a distance you would struggle to tell them apart. But they were quite different personalities. David was quieter and more studious while Jack was more sociable, talkative and outgoing.

'What have you got there, David?' asked Jack, slightly peeved that his brother, at 12 months younger than him, should be able to read such things. It was incredibly boring of him, but also annoyingly impressive.

'It's one of mum's old history volumes from the loft,' he replied. 'It dates from 1844 and it's about the treasures and antiquities of England. It's rather interesting, I must say. I bet I'm the first person to study it properly in more than a century.'

At that moment, their mother appeared from the kitch-en. 'Well make sure you take good care of it, David,' she warned. 'It's a precious book which belonged to my great-great grandfather and I don't want it damaged.'

'Don't worry, mum, he's only pretending to read it,'

teased Jack. 'You know what he's like, he loves to make himself look important. He'll be getting out his Welsh teach yourself books next.'

'You're only jealous because you're a year older than me but nowhere near as intellectual as I am,' retorted David. 'I don't recall you making fun of Lou for speaking Welsh. For your information I think this old book is very interesting. Just because the pages are yellowed and the print is a bit small and fuzzy doesn't make it boring.'

'Ok then, smarty pants,' replied Jack, 'what's the highlight so far? Does it have a particularly fascinating analysis of an ancient burial mound or something?'

'Well, as a matter of fact, yes, there is a rather interesting piece about Anglo-Saxon treasures buried in two spots in the Staffordshire countryside. From the location of one of the sites, I would guess that might be what we now know as the Staffordshire Hoard,' said David, raising his voice slightly so their mother would hear from the kitchen.

'Oh is that right,' said Jack, irritated at David's supercilious manner. 'Well don't get too excited – that was dug up and accounted for several years ago.'

'Maybe so, but it is curious that they appeared to know about its existence in 1844,' said David.

At that point their mother reappeared from the kitchen, intrigued by the conversation in the living room.

'That's impossible, David,' Mrs Johnson said. 'No-one knew anything of the Staffordshire Hoard until a metal detector enthusiast stumbled across it by accident in 2009 and it was all recovered from a single site, not two.'

'What exactly is the Staffordshire Hoard anyway,' enquired Jack, 'a big pile of dinosaur bones or something?'

'No, don't be silly, Jack,' said Mrs Johnson, who knew a great deal about history. 'The Staffordshire Hoard was the name given to a large quantity of beautifully-crafted items of Anglo-Saxon gold and silver. It was one of the biggest and best finds ever discovered in England. It dates back to the days when the Angles and Saxons came over from Germany many hundreds of years ago, shortly after Roman rule collapsed. Members of an Anglo-Saxon tribe buried the treasure in land near the village of Hammerwich near Lichfield in Staffordshire.

It was found by chance in 2009 by a man using a metal detector – which beeps when it senses metal below ground. The hoard was dug up and bought by museums for a great deal of money, which was shared between the finder and the farmer who owned the land. Certainly no-one previously knew of its whereabouts. I'm afraid David is letting his imagination run away with him.'

'There you are,' said Jack, triumphantly. 'I knew you were talking rubbish again, David. An account of the Staffordshire Hoard indeed, from a book written in 1844.'

'I didn't say it *was* the Staffordshire Hoard, merely that the location and description seem to tally,' replied David, defensively.

He fell silent. There was no point allowing himself to be rattled by Jack, who would always win any such tussle, whether he deserved to or not.

'Mum,' called David, in the direction of the kitchen to which his mother had returned. 'May I have a look at your book on the Staffordshire Hoard, now that I'm really interested in it?'

'Yes,' she called back, 'but make sure you take good care of it.'

Jack snorted in derision as David took it off the shelf and sat back down, now with two big, heavy books open across his lap.

'Hmm, *most* intriguing,' he announced, a few minutes later.

'Only to you though, David, so keep it to yourself,' bickered Jack, who was becoming fed up and fractious that day. He was missing Lou more than he cared to admit.

David didn't reply, he was too absorbed in his research. The description of buried treasure published in 1844 certainly did bear remarkable similarities to the account of the Staffordshire Hoard in the modern book. More to the point, the place where the hoard was found in 2009 – the north-west corner of a field in the parish of Hammerwich, just south of the Roman Road of Watling Street – seemed to tie in with one of the locations mentioned in the old book, although the latter wasn't so specific.

The Victorian author had written:

'According to Anglo-Saxon manuscripts now kept safely by the British Museum, a vicious battle had ensued between two warring tribes and the victors stripped their enemy of all weapons and suits of armour. They took their swords to use again while their pommel caps and hilt plates were buried in a field south of the famous Roman Road of Watling Street. These too were of great value, made in part from gold and featuring the most delightful garnet inlays and intricate designs of interwoven animals.

'Sadly, the womenfolk of the defeated tribe were not spared either. They were deprived of their precious jewellery – delightful and exquisite brooches, pendants and necklaces, even ornately designed dress fittings. These and other sundry items were taken and buried in a second, smaller hoard on land to the north of an important Roman settlement a couple of miles further down Watling Street, in the parish of Wall. The exact spot is unknown, but it is believed to be somewhere to the east of a small lake, with a tiny island of trees in the middle.'

But surely both locations would have been dug up long ago if they were already known about? That was plain common-sense. According to the Victorian author, very considerable efforts had been made to search the two sites, and nothing had been found. He concluded, therefore, that everything had been removed, either by the Anglo-Saxons themselves, or by unknown persons subsequently.

Yet if the larger pile of the treasure to which he referred *was* what became known as the Staffordshire Hoard, his conclusion was wrong, since it had indeed remained in the ground waiting patiently to be found. Had people in the Victorian era simply given up searching for it? They wouldn't have had sophisticated metal detectors then, of course. Also, an authoritative work like this, which no doubt carried great weight in its day, would surely have convinced most readers that it was already long gone.

David turned his attention to his mother's shiny modern book telling the story of the Staffordshire Hoard, illustrated with numerous photographs of the 3,500 items unearthed in 2009. A total of 5.094 kilos of gold and 1.442 kilos of silver had been excavated from the field in Hammerwich, believed to date from the 7th or 8th centuries. The old book had said the 8th century.

Yet was there any reference to a second site in the modern write-up? David could find nothing to suggest that. Then his heart skipped a beat, for he read:

'The two most striking features of the Staffordshire Hoard are that it is unbalanced, and it is of exceptionally high quality. It is unbalanced because of what is missing. There is absolutely nothing feminine. There are no dress fittings, brooches or pendants. These are the gold objects most commonly found from the Anglo-Saxon era. The vast majority of items in the hoard are martial – war gear, especially sword fittings.'

Surely, the fact that it was 'incomplete' would point to the possible existence of a second hoard, as indicated in the 1844 book? David scoured page after page of the modern text for any reference to it but there was nothing. Did today's archaeologists not even know that a second hoard was once believed to have been buried to the north of Watling Street, a couple of miles east from the discovery in 2009? Perhaps not.

Possibly, these insights printed in small, smudged type in an old book from Victorian times gathering dust in their loft had long been forgotten. How many other copies even still existed? The question was, reasoned David, if the Victorian author was right about one location, could he also be right about the second? Might it remain intact, still holding on to its riches?

David glanced at Jack, itching to share his thoughts with him. His brother was in an uncharacteristically bad mood that day. He sat there, scrapbook on his lap, gazing despondently out of the window.

'Hey Jack, how do you fancy going on the trail of buried treasure?'

'Don't be daft, David,' replied his brother, eventually.

'Listen, this old book says that there were two Anglo-Saxon hoards of treasure buried in Staffordshire,' said David, earnestly, 'if the Staffordshire Hoard was one and has been dug up, then perhaps the other is still in the ground.'

Jack yawned. 'Does the old book say the treasure is still there?'

'Er no, it says that it's most likely long since gone.'

Jack laughed. 'If the treasure had already disappeared by 1844, it's not likely to have reappeared since, is it?'

David attempted to explain his theory but then sighed in exasperation. Jack was having none of it.

'You're clutching at straws, David. Are you seriously suggesting we go all the way over there hunting for treasure in some farmer's field based on a book from 1844 which states categorically that the treasure isn't there any more? It's a fool's hope. Fool's gold!' he added with a smug grin.

'Do you know who you sound like?' said David. 'You sound like me, Jack. That is how I used to talk, but our adventure with Lou has changed me. What would Lou say about this? She'd say we find a way of getting over there and searching for it. Well, wouldn't she?'

'David there is no way that Lou would want to go on this sort of wild goose chase,' said Jack, his voice trailing off. The brothers looked at each other.

'There's only one way to find out, isn't there?' said David.

Jack paused for a few seconds. 'Ok look, I'll text her. I'll see what she says. We've still got a week before we go back to school so I suppose we could camp in a field nearby and use that as our base. We'd have to see if we could borrow a metal detector from someone.'

'Hang on,' said David, amused at Jack's sudden change of heart. 'I thought you said it was a crazy idea?'

'It *is* a crazy idea,' insisted Jack. 'But I suppose hunting for treasure could still be fun, provide Lou agrees to come too.'

David smiled as Jack went off to find his mobile phone. Of course! Jack wasn't remotely convinced by what he had said, but would gladly seek out a pot of gold beneath the end of a rainbow so long as Lou Elliott was alongside him. Mind you, so would he. The big question was, would she be interested in joining them and would their mums and dads agree? And would Emily be willing to go off on such an escapade, so soon after their thrilling, and at times scary, brush with smugglers?

CHAPTER TWO

Lou agrees to come

JACK paced the room, glancing every now and then at his mobile phone, willing it to ring or beep with a text message. The prospect of seeing Lou again and going camping had won him over completely.

'While we're waiting to hear back from her, shall we ask mum and dad if they'll agree? It's a non-starter if they don't,' he said.

'Let's see what Lou says first,' replied David. 'If she is on for it, let me be the one to ask permission. In fact, I'll just ask dad. You know how he always sees me as the boring, unadventurous one who never goes anywhere or does anything – chances are he'll be so impressed that I'm being more outgoing he'll agree.'

'Good idea,' agreed Jack. 'Meanwhile, why don't we have a think about where we would stay – we can't pitch our tents in the middle of a farmer's field without permission and nor can we hunt for treasure without permission, either. Why don't we try and find the spot on a map – we could look on the internet – and then see if there's a campsite nearby.'

David nodded and went to poke his head round the kitchen door. 'Mum, can I use the computer for a minute? I'm doing some research into the Staffordshire Hoard.'

'Ok David, you'll be quite an expert at this rate,' replied his mother, brushing her hands down her apron and looking amused. She was busy getting the Sunday roast prepared.

The boys went into the study and switched on the computer. David placed his two archaeology books down alongside.

‘I’ve just thought, where’s Emily this morning?’ said Jack. ‘She needs to be in on this from the start. It’s not fair to leave her out.’

‘Of course,’ replied David. ‘Go and find her while I get the internet up.’

Emily was in her bedroom engrossed in an adventure book. She had really got into her reading since meeting Lou at Abersoch. If an exciting, interesting person like Lou found books so appealing, then that was good enough for her. What’s more, she had developed rather a taste for adventure since their thrilling quest to uncover the activities of smugglers along the Lleyn peninsula of North Wales.

That had been a little too thrilling in places, of course. There were times when she had been frightened. From now on, she told herself, the only adventures she was interested in were those to be found within the pages of novels. That would be much more relaxing!

‘Emily, come downstairs for a minute,’ shouted Jack from the bottom of the staircase.

‘I’m reading my book. What do you want?’ shouted back Emily, irritated at the interruption.

‘David and I have come up with an exciting plan and we need your help.’

‘Well I’m in the middle of an exciting book,’ replied Emily, determined not to budge.

Jack bounded up the stairs and into her room.

‘Come on, Em, never mind about books, we’ve got some real-life fun for you. How do you fancy going camping again and seeking out buried treasure?’

‘Oh no way, we’ve been captured once searching for hidden loot this summer. I don’t fancy going through that experience again just yet.’

‘This will be different, Em,’ said Jack, earnestly. He always chummily called her “Em” when he wanted a favour from her. ‘This time, there won’t be any baddies to worry about – just the four of us, back together again, enjoying a camping holiday and searching for treasure. We wouldn't want to go without you. Why don't you come downstairs and we'll tell you all about it. You may not want to come, but you certainly won't want to be left out.'

'The four of us? Is Lou coming too?'

Her bright blue eyes looked intently at her brother's face.

'Yes, hopefully, that's the plan.'

'Ok, tell me more about it,' she sighed, closing her book and following Jack down the stairs.

Jack and Emily found David hunched over the computer. The image of a smallish field was displayed on the screen.

'You see where the ground looks as though it's been disturbed,' said David, turning round. He always enjoyed imparting information to the others. 'Well that's the exact site of the Staffordshire Hoard. It was in that field, just below the old Roman Road of Watling Street, now the modern A5, where piles of gold and silver were dug up in 2009. And all because of a lucky strike with a metal detector.'

'Now,' he continued, 'that's the site everyone knows about. It contained only male, military items. According to the Victorian book, the precious family belongings and women's jewellery missing from the main hoard were buried a couple of miles further down Watling Street in the parish of Wall. The spot is just to the north of the road and somewhere to the east of a small lake, with a tiny island of trees in the middle. I think I've found the place they mean.'

David clicked out of the aerial photograph he had called up on Google Maps, then zoomed in on a lake in a field a short distance to the east. It had a small island of trees in the middle and appeared to match the description perfectly. Emily seemed impressed and David looked pleased with himself.

'That certainly looks like it might be the right spot, but that doesn't mean the treasure is still there to find, does it?' said Emily.

'No it doesn't,' admitted David. 'The old book claimed that the treasure had been removed from both locations but like I've explained to Jack, if it was wrong about one it might be wrong about both. Anyway there is surely no harm in us going along and swishing a metal detector across the land near to that lake. What do you say, Emily?'

'Hmm,' said Emily, glancing at Jack. 'At a guess, Jack thinks your plan is pretty far-fetched but he just sees it as a good excuse to meet up with Lou again.'

'I don't see any harm in looking for this treasure,' said Jack, 'if it means we can do a spot of camping in the fresh air in the last few days before the autumn term starts. After all, look at us, we're bored and irritable again and missing being with Lou.'

'Well as a matter of fact, I was enjoying reading a jolly good book,' replied Emily. 'But yes, I suppose it would be fun to go over there. So is Lou up for it? What about the small matter of getting ourselves a metal detector and where exactly we would camp?'

'I haven't heard back from Lou yet,' admitted Jack, rather despondently. 'I'm sure she'll be keen.'

'Right, well I'm going back to my exciting book, let me know if you hear from her,' said Emily, heading for the stairs. Before she got half way up, Jack's phone beeped loudly, making them jump.

'It's Lou!' exclaimed Jack.

Her message was characteristically brief and to the point. 'Sounds interesting – will need proper organising. Will call u in a bit, Lou.'

A few minutes later, his phone rang. The name 'Lou

Elliott' flashed up on the display. Jack was so excited to speak to her for the first time since their adventure in Abersoch that he gabbled and could barely make himself understood.

'Right, put David on,' said Lou, impatiently, 'since he is the brains behind it all.'

Somewhat crestfallen, Jack passed the phone to his brother who took great delight in explaining his theory about a second, long-forgotten Staffordshire Hoard and why it really might still be in the ground after all this time, even though the Victorians had given up on it. He had got his little talk on the subject off to a fine art by now.

'Where will we camp and where do you propose to find a metal detector,' replied Lou, curtly, echoing Emily's concerns. Lou had had yet another row with her parents that morning and was in no mood to be bowled over by airy-fairy ideas from Jack and David.

Lou was a shrewd, intelligent girl with vivid green eyes looking out from beneath a fringe of dark hair. The others had her to thank for getting them out of some tight corners during their brush with smugglers in North Wales. Although arguably, it was she who had got them into those tight corners in the first place.

'Er, well, we haven't got quite that far yet,' said David. 'We were about to look into that.'

'Ok, let me have a think about how we can do it and I'll get back to you,' said Lou. 'We can't just pitch our tents in a farmer's field and start digging it up. Leave it with me and I'll ring you back later.'

'Will your parents be ok about you coming?' said David.

'Oh don't worry about them, they won't care one way or the other.'

'And Lou, do you definitely think it's worth a shot?' added David, almost pleadingly.

'Yes I do, speak later.'

With that, she was gone. Lou didn't do long telephone conversations. The boys didn't mind. They looked at each other exultantly. Lou not only wanted to come, she actually thought there might be something in it!

Lou gazed from her bedroom window towards the bleak, beautiful hill country known as the Long Mynd. Her family home in rural Shropshire looked out onto its lower slopes. Lou would spend hours walking across its moors and along its tinkling streams and grassy paths. Usually, she would go off on her own. She had no brothers or sisters and few friends living locally, so holidays were often quite lonely experiences. She never minded much, but meeting the Johnson family at Abersoch made her realise that it was good to spend time in the company of others. She'd really enjoyed meeting Jack, David and Emily and leading them on the hunt for smugglers.

Lou had been sad when their time together came to an end and the Johnsons headed back home. She and her parents stayed on for another week at their holiday cottage but it wasn't the same somehow. It would be great to see the others again.

As for seeking to find the missing hoard of Anglo-Saxon treasure which had apparently already vanished by the 1840s – well, why not? Lou didn't think that David's theory was necessarily daft. If anything, it struck her as plausible. Certainly it was worth a try. The worst that could happen was that they wouldn't find anything. Also, she was badly missing the others, particularly scatter-brained Jack. Going camping with them would be a fun way of spending the final week of the summer holidays.

Trouble is, thought Lou, I'm going to be the one who's expected to take charge and organise everything. At least her parents were out for the day so she had plenty of time to plan and use her father's laptop without him getting cross. She would also need to fish out his metal detector from beneath a pile of junk in the garage. Mr Elliott had bought it a couple of years ago – the latest in a long line of expensive electronic gadgets he simply had to have, only to lose interest in soon afterwards. No wonder he and her mother were short of money.

Within minutes Lou had called up an online map of the field where the Staffordshire Hoard had been excavated. Then she scrolled the map eastwards until she came upon the second site – the field just north of Watling Street containing a small, tree-covered lake. She stared in fascination at the mottled-green expanse of land alongside it. It looked like ordinary grazing pasture or a field of crops. It was astonishing to think what might lie beneath a row of cabbages without anyone having the remotest idea. The thought made her spine tingle.

She was tempted to research the Staffordshire Hoard but decided not to. David would not appreciate anyone seeking to rival his expertise in the matter. It was best left to him. What she needed to do was to sort out the practicalities. Where would they camp, and would the farmer who owned the land let them loose across his fields, waving a metal detector about?

Interestingly, the field with the lake in it looked to belong to a different farm from the site of the Staffordshire Hoard. That was a good thing – the landowner wouldn't have reaped any reward from it and might perhaps welcome a little extra income from a group of campers.

Lou zoomed in on what looked like farm buildings and called up Google Street View. The farm name and telephone number could clearly be seen on a metal sign attached to the side of a barn adjacent to the lane running through the parish of Wall. It said: P. Owen, Home Farm, and it had a telephone number underneath.

She reached for her mobile phone and began tapping the number in, but then stopped herself. She needed to decide what to say first, and how open it was wise to be about their wish to search for treasure. It was, she decided, only fair to be totally straight with the farmer or his wife and to explain exactly what they hoped to do.

Her instinct served her well. It was the farmer himself who answered and he guffawed with a rich, hearty laugh upon hearing Lou's strange request.

'So,' he said, 'let's get this straight. You want to pitch your tents in my fields and search around the shores of the lake for buried treasure? Well you're in luck, I've harvested and ploughed the land adjacent to the lake recently and it's just soil and stubble, so you can't do too much damage. It will be much easier for you to dig it, too.

'Also, ploughing can often throw up interesting items from long ago. You won't be able to camp on it, mind, I'll have to find you some flat grass for that. There will be four of you, you say, all youngsters? Well I never, we don't often get requests like this. Hold the line for a tick, I'll ask the wife.'

A minute or so later, and the farmer was back on. 'She says it's fine so long as your parents are happy and give their permission. Tell you the truth, it will be useful money for us, my dairy business is struggling a bit at the moment. Oh and missie, remember the old rule that treasure hunters must abide by – any finds are split 50-50 with the landowner! I must say I was green with envy when farmer Fred Johnson from across the way made his fortune from the Staffordshire Hoard.'

Lou chuckled. That lucky farmer had the same surname as Jack, David and Emily – perhaps that was a good omen!

'Well let's not get our hopes up,' she said. 'But I faithfully promise you that we'll share anything we find with you.'

Mr Owen bawled with laughter again and Lou found herself warming to him – he sounded a decent, down-to-earth sort of chap, which most farmers were, of course. Now all they had to do was to convince their parents to let them go. Her own mum and dad wouldn't be a problem, they had let their only daughter run wild long ago. Mr and Mrs Johnson would be more of a challenge, however. Probably best if I speak to them myself, thought Lou.

They certainly did take a lot of persuading. David had got in first and flown into a childish rage when his mum and dad started to make objections and express concern that they hadn't thought things through properly.

Their house phone rang. It was Lou, calling them direct. Mrs Johnson listened in admiration and some astonishment as the 12-year-old calmly briefed them on the arrangements she had already made with farmer Mr Owen.

'If you have any concerns, why don't you ring him yourself,' said Lou, 'he sounds a nice chap. And you know me, Mrs Johnson, I'll look after Jack, David and Emily like I did at Abersoch. They'll come to no harm with me at their side.'

Hmm, thought Mrs Johnson. Headstrong, feisty Lou was the perfect ally for anyone who got into a scrape – it's just that she was the sort of mischief-maker who might well put them in that scrape in the first place. But she and her husband Paul had become very fond of Lou during their holiday at Abersoch and had seen the transformation she had brought about in their dull, stay-at-home children, particularly David.

'Ok, Lou,' said Mrs Johnson. 'I'll have a word with Mr Owen and his wife and if they sound like trustworthy people, I will agree to you going.'

A few minutes later, Jack and David were leaping around the room in delight, cheering and shouting. Emily, clutching her Kindle to her chest, came out of her bedroom to find out what the fuss was about.

'We're off on a camping expedition with Lou,' yelled Jack, up the stairs. 'It's going to be brilliant!'

'Hey, not just camping – don't forget my buried treasure,' shouted David.

'Ah ha, me hearties, pieces of eight, pieces of eight!' said Jack, theatrically.

Mr Johnson, who had walked in from the garden, grinned at his sons. He wasn't too worried by the whole idea so long as someone capable like Lou was in charge. This was how he was at their age, wanting to get out and explore the world. With the racket they were making, the sooner they headed south to Staffordshire and gave him a bit of peace, the better!

CHAPTER THREE

Off camping

MR and Mrs Johnson had offered to drive their children to Wall in Staffordshire but they insisted on going by train, taking their bikes with them. They would meet Lou off her train at Lichfield City railway station, then cycle the last stretch.

The following day, the last Saturday in August, dawned bright and sunny. Mum and dad helped get them organised with two smallish tents – one for the boys to sleep in and the other for the girls. By 8.25am, Jack, David and Emily were waving goodbye to their parents as their train pulled away from the platform at Whitchurch station. They were all extremely excited to be making their own way to Staffordshire.

It made them feel very grown up and independent. They had to change trains twice, at Crewe then at Lichfield Trent Valley. That added greatly to the fun. Grown-ups hate having to change trains but children love it. They were due to arrive at Lichfield City at 10.23.

'A whole two hours of train journey – fantastic!' enthused Jack.

'I don't suppose Lou will end up on the same train, will she?' asked Emily, 'after all, she's travelling from Shropshire and so are we.'

'Yes,' said David, 'but we are travelling from the north of Shropshire near the border with Cheshire, and she's coming from the other end of the county.

'She was catching the train from Church Stretton at about five past eight,' said Jack. 'She will change trains at Shrewsbury and Birmingham New Street and arrive at Lichfield at 10.32 – nine minutes after us.'

'Poor Lou, having half an hour longer on the train and all by herself, I hope she'll be ok,' said Emily, looking worried.

'Don't be daft Emily,' replied Jack. 'Of course Lou will be ok, she's not exactly the sort to be frightened of travelling alone, is she? I can't wait to see her again – we had such a good time with her at Abersoch.'

'Yes we did,' said Emily, 'but it was a bit scary, too. I don't want to be held prisoner again and tied up.'

'It won't be anything like that,' insisted Jack. 'Last time we stumbled across the activities of smugglers, went on their trail and got tangled up with them. This time, we are searching for buried treasure which the world has long forgotten about. We'll camp in a farmer's field in a sleepy rural village with not a single baddie on the horizon. What could be more relaxing?'

'Jack's right. Nothing could possibly go wrong and we won't come into any danger,' reassured David. 'Just think of it as a fun camping holiday in the fresh air which will be a great way to finish the summer holidays.'

The two boys spent the rest of the train journey nattering excitedly and gazing out of the window as the train passed through the pleasant farmland of north Staffordshire, bound for the cathedral city of Lichfield.

'Just think,' said David, 'any one of those fields we can see through the window could hold long-lost Anglo-Saxon treasure.'

'The question is,' said Jack, 'will there be any beneath the field we are going to search? You really are going to get teased about this David, if we don't find so much as an antique coat button or anything.'

'Well remember what you said when we were at Abersoch and I told you I'd overheard smugglers talking about a buried case on the island in the bay. Nobody believed me – but within a day . . . '

'Very true,' said Jack, his freckly face bursting into a

smile. 'That was the start of our amazing adventure. I don't care what we find – I'm so pleased we're off again for a second holiday with Lou without a grown-up in sight. I didn't think we'd be seeing her for ages. Whatever happens it will be loads of fun, and somehow with Lou leading the way, my guess is something interesting will happen.'

David nodded while Emily's soft blue eyes looked up from her book at her two brothers with a touch of apprehension in them.

The train chugged into Lichfield City station bang on time at 10.23. The guard helped the children off the train with their bikes and bulky rucksacks.

'You look all set for an expedition,' he said, with a grin.

'Oh you can say that again,' replied David. 'We're off camping and exploring and we're going to have a great time.'

The guard gave them a cheery wave as he jumped back on the train. 'Wish I could come,' he shouted ruefully.

Jack paced up and down the platform looking at his watch. It felt like a very long nine minutes and in fact to his dismay, Lou's connection from Birmingham was running two minutes late, according to the big electronic sign.

'Oh don't panic Jack, she'll be here before you know it,' said David. 'While we're waiting, let's have a look at the map I printed out. I've marked the route from Lichfield to Wall in red pen. Hang on, I know it's in here somewhere.'

Several minutes passed and David was unable to find the map, despite rummaging valiantly through the many pockets of his rucksack.

'Oh you're hopeless, David, I might have known we couldn't rely on you,' reproached his brother. 'We'll have to hope that Lou has got a map or something. Oh look, that's her train now!'

Sure enough the train from Birmingham was pulling up at the platform. Jack and David raced over, leaving their rucksacks and bikes propped against the bench. Wisely, Emily stayed put to look after them.

'Lou!' shouted Jack as the unmistakeable figure of Louise Elliott alighted gracefully from the middle carriage. She looked prettier and more striking than ever in her smart polka dot jacket, sequinned jeans and white trainers. She'd had her hair trimmed since they'd last seen her, more of a bob although her fringe still came down to her eyes.

'Boys, give me a hug!' exclaimed Lou as they came up to her. Neither needed asking twice. 'It's great to see you again. Give me a hand will you.'

Jack grabbed her rucksack and David began wheeling her bike.

'Oh I'm glad to be off that train,' said Lou. 'It was lovely through Shropshire but the train from Birmingham was full of all sorts of annoying people and continual loudspeaker announcements. Still, we'll soon be off on our bikes, cycling through some wonderful countryside.'

Emily got up and smiled bashfully as Lou approached. She felt in awe of her and a good deal younger – which she was of course, by a good two years.

'Hello Emily,' said Lou, giving her a big hug and a kiss on the cheek. 'So glad you're here to help me keep your brothers in check. So this was your daft idea was it, David?'

David looked rather disappointed at her. He had taken an awful lot of leg-pulling over his buried treasure theory – from Jack, mum, Emily and now Lou!

Lou grinned cheerily at him and gave his shoulder a friendly punch.

'Hey, I think it's brilliant and well worth checking out.

Apart from anything else, it's got the gang reunited hasn't it? There was me thinking I wouldn't see you again this side of Christmas and here we are again. It's a shame there are no beaches and no sea but it looks like we're off to an idyllic spot surrounded by lovely country lanes we can cycle along. I can't wait to get going with our metal detector and spades!'

'Erm Lou,' said Jack, nervously. 'You did say you were bringing a metal detector didn't you, only you don't appear to have it with you.'

The others looked at her with dismayed faces.

'Oh it's a good thing one of us organised this expedition properly isn't it?' retorted Lou, her emerald eyes flashing a mixture of annoyance and amusement. 'No I haven't got the metal detector with me because it's a great big thing with headphones you have to wear and I couldn't manage that and my rucksack and ride a bike. Oh and did anyone think about bringing spades?'

The others looked blank.

'Well how do you think we will dig anything up if the metal detector beeps to say there's something in the ground?'

'I think we erm, thought you would probably sort it out, Lou,' mumbled Emily, while the boys sheepishly said nothing.

'You don't say!' grinned Lou wickedly. 'I have, of course. My dad has parcelled up the metal detector and sent it to the farm – we simply pick it up when we get there. As for spades, the farmer Mr Owen has kindly offered to lend us some, and trowels and garden forks if we want them.'

The others looked relieved.

'Where would we be without you?' said Jack.

'In a fix,' retorted Lou, somewhat unkindly. 'Now, have you got a map we can follow to get from here to Wall? I estimate it will be less than three miles, so we should make it in half an hour or so.'

'Erm, I thought I had – I erm, printed one out off the computer and I put it ready to take but I think I might have left it behind,' stuttered David, blushing.

'Right,' said Lou, avoiding the temptation to make David feel any worse. 'Let's use mine shall we?'

She pulled it out of her inside pocket, carefully wrapped in cling-film in case of rain, with the route highlighted with bright yellow marker pen.

'It should be a lovely ride once we get out of Lichfield and onto Claypit Lane,' said Lou. 'I love cycling along country lanes.'

'You know, I almost feel like we're back at Abersoch,' exclaimed Jack as the four of them pedalled speedily along Claypit Lane which was barely wide enough for cars.

'Yes,' agreed David. 'It feels to me like that day when we cycled off to Whistling Sands. That was such a lovely day out.'

'It's picturesque round here,' said Lou. 'Miles of rolling farmland all around and clusters of huge big trees. It's not got the savage beauty of North Wales, but it's a gentle, pastoral scene. Reminds me a lot of Shropshire.

'Oh and do you remember,' continued Lou, who was leading the way, confident she knew the route from memory, 'that day we cycled to Whistling Sands we were hoping to find clues about the smugglers, but in fact we found nothing and then, when we least expected it, we saw one of them that evening back in Abersoch when we were out having a pub meal. And you, David, were the hero of the hour – tracking him back to his dingy hotel.'

David grinned at the memory while Emily couldn't resist saying that she hoped they wouldn't come across any baddies this time.

'Don't you worry, Emily,' said Lou. 'There won't be a

baddy in sight this time!'

'Oh wow, look at that enormous field full of bright yellow flowers,' exclaimed Emily as they rounded a bend. 'Doesn't that look amazing!'

'It's rapeseed oil,' said Lou, knowledgeably. 'A lot of farmers grow it these days, the flowers produce oil which can be used in cooking and even as a fuel. This must be a late crop, it's usually harvested in June. It does look dramatic with the sun shining on it, doesn't it? I'm not sure what I think of it though. It's too garish for me.'

'Hey look ahead – the sign for Wall! We're here already!' said Lou. 'That didn't take long did it?'

The youngsters looked about them approvingly as they cycled into the village. Huge horse chestnut trees towered above them to their right, while on their left were half a dozen or so pleasant, tidy-looking semi-detached houses in red brick with neat front gardens.

'Now to find the farm,' declared Lou. 'It shouldn't be that difficult.'

It wasn't. Within a few seconds, they came across Home Farm on the right.

'Ok,' said Lou. 'We better go and introduce ourselves and find out where we can camp.'

They dismounted from their bikes as they entered the farmyard. Emily felt on edge. A sheepdog was sitting in the back of an open truck. It pricked up its ears and growled and whined slightly upon seeing them. Then it raised its muzzle and howled.

Emily began to back away but the others stood their ground.

'It's ok Emily,' said Lou. 'Farm dogs always howl and bark when anyone strange comes into the farmyard. It helps keep the place safe. A flock of geese are good for that too.'

Right on cue, two geese appeared and started waddling over towards the youngsters, opening their beaks.

They were more menacing than the dog and the children were somewhat relieved when a plumpish, cheery-faced woman appeared from the farmhouse and approached them.

'Ah you must be the Johnson children and Miss Louise Elliott of course, whom I spoke to on the phone,' she said with a smile. 'I'm Mrs Owen, welcome to Home Farm, we hope you'll enjoy your stay here. We're a proper, old-fashioned farm and if you have time free after your treasure hunting to have a good look round then you'd be most welcome.'

'I'm Lou,' said Lou, introducing herself.

'Hello Lou,' beamed Mrs Owen. 'I daresay you're the boss of the four of you!' she added, shrewdly, noticing how confident Lou seemed, in contrast to the shyness of the others.

'I'm the chief troublemaker you might say,' replied Lou, grinning. 'These are my friends Jack, David and Emily and as you can see, we've come on our bikes and we've got all our camping gear.'

'It's lovely to meet you all,' said Mrs Owen. 'Your metal detector arrived this morning, all parcelled up, and my husband will supply you with spades.

'Now, if you need eggs, milk, cheese, bacon and such like, you come and ask me for it. I've arranged with your parents to send them the bill so don't worry about paying – not that I'll be charging much, I just want to make sure you don't go hungry while you're here. There's a little shop and post office in the village where you can buy most other things.

'I'm afraid there's not that much in the way of entertainment out here, but Lichfield's not that far away of course if you want to go there and do a spot of shopping and sight-seeing. It's a picturesque place. We could always run you there if you didn't fancy cycling.'

'That's helpful of you, Mrs Owen,' said Lou. 'I don't

suppose we will want for much. We love the open countryside and if we can be out in the fresh air exploring and cycling around, we'll be happy enough. I've grown up in rural Shropshire, near the Long Mynd, so I'm used to being in the middle of nowhere.'

'We live in quite a small village in Cheshire,' said Jack, finding his tongue at last, 'and we love the countryside too.'

'It sounds like you'll be fine here,' said Mrs Owen, beaming again. 'Now why don't you come into the farmhouse for some breakfast and we'll find that husband of mine. He can take you to the place where you're to camp and show you the way to our little lake that you're interested in.'

The children gladly followed Mrs Owen into the huge farmhouse kitchen. It was laid with big red quarry tiles with a sturdy if rather battered pine table in the middle.

'Now you take a seat and I'll get you a good hearty plateful, to give you plenty of energy for your treasure hunting,' chortled Mrs Owen. 'Don't get your hopes up too high, mind, it was a chance in a million that those metal detector folk found the Hoard across the way. I doubt we'll see the likes of that again round these parts, not for many a long year.'

'Well whatever we find, we'll share with you Mrs Owen,' piped up Emily, smiling warmly at her. Emily's sparkling blue eyes seemed filled with a cheery calm now that they had arrived and Mrs Owen had turned out to be so welcoming. Her misgivings had largely been dispelled and she was beginning to feel rather pleased at the prospect of a camping holiday.

'Aah you're a sweetie,' replied the farmer's wife. 'There's more charm in you than my sulky daughter I'll tell you that much. She's a stubborn one and no mistake. Mind you, I'm hoping she'll grow out of it. Now, there's bacon, sausage, fried egg, black pudding, tomato, mushrooms, potato cakes, plenty of bubble and squeak and toast and marmalade to follow. And a nice hot cup of tea of course. Any of that you don't fancy, now's the time to say.'

'Sounds like the best breakfast ever,' said David approvingly, as a huge plateful was put in front of him.

'Well you'll be living off what you can cook on a camping stove for the next few days, so this should get you off to a good start,' said Mrs Owen. 'You can always come in for a plateful of hot food if you fancy it. That's one thing we're never short of on a farm, is food.'

'Or talkative women,' said the big, deep voice of her husband, striding into the kitchen in his muddy gloves and matching muddy boots.

'Oh Peter,' scolded his wife. 'Just look at the mess you're making. I only swept this floor half an hour ago. A woman's work is never done – you'll find that out one day,' said Mrs Owen to Lou and Emily.

'Now take those filthy gloves and boots off and sit down at the table or there'll be no breakfast for you,' she said, turning back to her husband. Show some manners and say hello to our guests.'

'Hello youngsters,' said Mr Owen, his weather-beaten stubbly face breaking into a grin beneath a generous tangle of dark hair. 'I'm afraid graceful table manners aren't my strong point. Saying that, you don't get cows milked and pigs fed and crops sown on good manners.'

'That's no excuse for not having any,' tutted his wife. 'Now get some food down you and behave yourself and then you can take the youngsters out with you and show them where they're to camp.'

'So,' said Mr Owen, his mouth half full of black pudding, 'tell me the exciting tale of the second Staffordshire Hoard, I'm dying to know!'

David, blushing slightly, gave a nervous cough and then embarked on a rather dry and long-winded account of how the antique archaeology book from his parents' loft had led him to believe there just might be a long-forgotten hoard of treasure buried near the lake on Mr Owen's land.

Lou listened a touch uneasily. Were they giving too much away? Ought they to be so candid with the farmer who seemed pretty curious. She shrugged off such misgivings. He was the landowner after all, and arguably anything found belonged to him far more so than to them.

Mr Owen roared with laughter when David had finished. 'You'll find not much more than a few rusty old farm tools and buried fence wire most likely,' he said. 'But why on earth not have a jolly good look. I think it's great you've got enough spirit and sense of adventure to come here on your own like this and follow your dream. Good luck to you, I say!'

'Well, like I've told your wife, Mr Owen, whatever we find,' said Emily, her blue eyes looking earnestly at him, 'we faithfully promise to share it with you – even if it's no more than a rusty old can.'

'Hey let's hope you find two rusty old cans,' hooted Mr Owen, 'then you can keep one and we'll keep the other!'

Everyone burst out laughing. That is, everyone save for a sullen-looking face which had suddenly appeared in the doorway.

'Are these the treasure hunters,' sneered a girl who looked older than Jack and Lou – and somehow younger at the same time. 'I don't see why they should keep anything they find, if it's on our land.'

Lou and the others looked at her with unease. They had begun to feel so welcome and content. It was a shame if anything was going to spoil it.

'Because, darling daughter, that is what has happened since the dawn of time – finders keep half and the land-owner keeps half. It's been like that for centuries. This is Becky,' said Mr Owen turning to the others. 'She's our only child – thank goodness. Mind you, if she didn't scowl so much, she'd be quite pretty.'

Lou shot Becky a sharp and penetrating glance. Lou was good at seeing the real person, whatever they appeared to be on the outside. Instantly, she saw something of herself in her – a reminder of the many times she had been a sulky child herself in the past. She might still be if she hadn't made herself snap out of it. However, Lou hadn't had a great upbringing, with parents who didn't bother with her. What was Becky's excuse for being so pouty and hostile, she wondered?

Becky's big brown eyes logged Lou's stare and wrongly took it as a threat. This was a bad start. She curled her lip at her and sneered: 'you better keep out of my way. This is my home and I don't want to see you strangers poking your noses around it.'

'We won't get in your way,' replied Lou, calmly. 'You're welcome to come and help with the treasure hunt if you'd like and spent some time with us.'

'You've got to be kidding,' said Becky, and with a toss of her long, wavy chestnut locks, flounced out of the kitchen and disappeared.

'Take no notice of her,' said Mrs Owen, spotting Emily's worried face. 'She's an only child and doesn't mix easily with others I'm afraid. She both loves and hates living in the country. She gets desperately lonely but take her into town and she's overwhelmed and runs scared. She can't cope with lots of people around her but she's not a bad girl at heart, not a bad girl at all.'

'Now my friends,' said Mr Owen, with a loud clap of his big, powerful hands, 'how about you come with me in the jeep and we'll go off and set up base camp?'

The children, having scraped their plates clean, nodded and got up. The encounter with Becky had unsettled them and they were keen to get back into the fresh air.

'Thank you so much for that wonderful breakfast Mrs

Owen,' said Lou. She noticed that the woman looked pained and guessed that her daughter caused her quite a lot of worry.

'Give me a chance with Becky,' said Lou. 'I'd like her to come and spend some time with us, and I think I know how to handle her – you see, she's quite a lot like me. If a wild child like me can be tamed, then maybe so can your Becky.'

Mrs Owen looked gratefully at Lou. 'If you can tame that girl, you'll do a lot better than her own mother,' she said. 'It would do her good to have some company of her own age although I'm afraid there's more chance of you digging up gold than getting a smile out of her.'

'We can but try,' said Lou cheerfully, glancing at the others who looked less than enthusiastic at the prospect of doing any such thing.

Mr Owen lifted their bikes and rucksacks into the back of his truck.

'Jump on board – you can sit in the back if you like – it's not going to rain on you.'

The four of them jumped in and held on tight as it bumped its way down a farm track, passing a few more geese and an inquisitive pig along the way.

'To your left, you'll see a lovely field of ripening wheat,' shouted Mr Owen through the hatch. 'On your right, you'll see row upon row of big green plants. That's maize – or corn, if you're American.'

'Sweetcorn?' asked David.

'Depends when it's harvested,' replied the farmer. 'If you cut it down when the kernels are sweet, it's sweetcorn and you can eat it for you tea but if it's kept for longer, it hardens up and can be turned into flour or animal feed – all kinds of things.'

'I'd rather like to be a farmer I think,' said Jack, looking around him.

Mr Owen gave one of his hearty laughs. 'There's not

much money to be made in farming these days, I'm afraid. It's a tough life and long hours. I'm up at 4.30am milking and I'm working most days till the sun sets, and so's my wife.'

'Do you enjoy it, Mr Owen?' enquired Emily.

'I love it,' he replied. 'I was born into it remember and it's the only life I've known. Young folk like you, truth to tell, don't want to be bothered with farming – too much hard work for too little reward and I can't say as I blame anyone for thinking like that. We've enough money to get by, working dawn till dusk, but there are easier ways to make a living, believe me. I'll certainly be pleased if you find buried treasure, that would be the answer to all our prayers!'

'We'll do our best for you,' said Emily, 'that's a promise.'

'You do that missie,' said the farmer, looking round and grinning. 'Well, here we are – this is where I propose for you to camp.'

Mr Owen pulled up half-way into a grass field bordered by hedgerows. Huge oaks, ash and chestnut trees were dotted around the field and, towards the end, several formed a loose circle.

'Now you can pitch your tents wherever you like in this field, it's flat enough, but my suggestion would be to put them up inside that circle of poplars yonder,' said Mr Owen, pointing. 'It will be nicely sheltered should the wind get up and I've stuck a few old flat tree stumps in the middle which you can use to sit on.'

They got out and strolled inside the poplar trees – a good-sized patch of lush grass formed a pleasant glade. The tree-stump seats dotted about would prove useful for campfire meals. There was plenty of room for their two tents and space too, for a cooking area in the middle. They had brought with them a couple of small outdoor stoves to heat a kettle of water and a nest of small pans.

'Now, you'll be wondering where you can get water from. You see that outbuilding over there,' said Mr Owen, pointing back through the trees the way they had come, 'that's got an outside tap which is fresh, drinkable water. Fill your water bottles with that whenever you like. Or you'll find a stream running along the eastern edge of the field and that is pure, fresh water but you might want to boil it before you drink it.

'There are also washing facilities in that outbuilding which you can use any time or you might want to bathe in the lake – it's crystal clear and perfectly safe.'

'So where is the lake from here then,' asked David, who was more curious than any of them to see with his own eyes the place near to the spot where Anglo-Saxon treasure might be buried.

'Right,' said Mr Owen. 'At the top of the field is a wooden gate. It's hard to see inside these poplar trees but go through that gate and you'll see a freshly-ploughed field. In the top left hand corner is the lake set in some rather nice trees and shrubs with a tiny island in the middle.

'So if your hunch is that the treasure is near that lake then you've got an empty ploughed field to stomp through – I'll be spreading it with muck and seeding it with winter wheat in a month so you've turned up in the nick of time!'

'Are we ok to dig wherever we like?' asked Lou.

'You can dig every square inch of it if it pleases you,' said the farmer. 'The more you dig, the better the soil will be so feel free. Ooh, that reminds me, your spades and forks and metal detector – they're still in the back of the truck – let's get them out now before I drive off with them again.'

The children helped Mr Owen lift everything out and carry them safely into their circular campsite.

'Here, have this tarpaulin as well,' said the farmer, you can keep your metal detector safely wrapped up in that at night so it doesn't get damp. The dew won't hurt the spades and forks but anything electrical is worth protecting.'

The others nodded. Mr Owen couldn't be more helpful and friendly. They gave him a cheery wave as he drove away and promised faithfully to call round if they needed help or ran out of supplies.

CHAPTER FOUR

Settling in

'YOU simply couldn't wish for a nicer couple,' said Lou, sitting on one of the tree stumps. 'It's such a stroke of luck because it's not as if they are used to having campers setting up on their fields.'

'Yes,' said Jack, 'it's a pity their daughter is such a moody, cross-looking thing. She didn't take to us at all.'

'The less we see of her the better,' chipped in David, who was himself hardly the most sociable of people.

'Don't be too quick to judge her,' replied Lou. 'Many people who seem frosty and unpleasant on the outside can be good souls once you get to know them – and some people who seem charming and friendly can be the opposite. That said, I think Mr and Mrs Owen are wonderful, I took to them straightaway.'

'You're a good judge of character Lou, what do you make of Becky then,' asked Emily. 'You surely can't see much to like in her?'

'Her problem is that she doesn't seem to like herself or believe in herself, for some reason,' said Lou. 'However, there is something about me in her, I can sense it. Whether she's a good egg or a bad egg though, I can't honestly say – she's a mystery. I think underneath, on balance, she's a good egg.'

'Either way, we shouldn't need to have too much to do with her,' said Jack, 'so much the better if you ask me.'

'Come on,' said Lou, 'let's get moving and get these tents put up. Then we'll get my mini stove lit under my tin kettle and have ourselves a cup of tea. Then we'll really feel we're on holiday again.' The others agreed. Once their tents were up they could relax.

'Now, the girls' tent can go here and why don't you boys put yours up there. It's perfectly flat ground. Come on, no slacking, these tents won't put up themselves!'

Jack, David and Emily looked on with admiration as Lou swiftly threaded the tent poles through the loops and a mass of messy canvas suddenly sprang to life as a tent.

'Come on you lot, don't just stand there,' she chided them. 'Either help me with this one or get the other one up.'

The others scurried around with the poles making rather a hash of it until Lou came over and showed them what to do. 'You must learn to put up a tent properly you know, it's an important skill.'

After about half an hour, two olive green tents were up on either side of the circle, with groundsheets down and sleeping bags unfurled. A camping stove was already alight with a kettle on it, filled with sparkling clear stream water.

'Doesn't this look like a simply wonderful little campsite,' enthused Emily, as she took a steaming tin mug of tea from Lou. 'I feel like I'm away on holiday again, like I did at Abersoch. Drinking tea out in the fresh air and surrounded by wonderful countryside.'

The others agreed. The farmer had found them an idyllic spot. To be camped in a circle of tall trees, swishing and swaying ever so gently in the light summer breeze with blue sky above and the magical sight of rolling hills peeping through the leaves. It was approaching midday now and the sun was high in the sky but with the whispering poplars all around the light was dappled and diffused – warm but not baking hot.

Through a gap in the swaying branches and leaves, the red brick farmhouse could be seen in the distance, glowing in the sunshine. The spire of the parish church poked up beyond it. On all sides could be seen field after field, far into the distance.

'Look over there,' said Emily, 'isn't that field beautiful – all golden in the sun with splodges of red in it.'

'They're poppies,' said Lou, sipping her tea, 'growing amidst ripening wheat. They come up by themselves, wherever they choose. Sometimes they can turn a whole field red. I love seeing them dancing in the breeze. Now, does anyone feel like any food or are we much too full?'

They were much too full. In fact, they didn't feel like doing anything, apart from pottering around amid the trees, cradling their tea mugs and breathing in the fragrant country air.

'You know what makes this camping holiday really special,' said Jack, looking at Lou, 'it's the fact that we are here totally by ourselves. Unlike at Abersoch, our parents are nowhere near, we are on our own and we never expected to be here. We were moping around at home, counting the days down to going back to school.'

'I was too,' said Lou. 'I was thrilled when you suggested we come here. It's great to be reunited again so soon. Once again we have David to thank.'

'Do we?' said Jack, slightly put out.

'Well yes,' said Lou. 'All this was David's idea based on his research. Who knows, maybe there is still treasure to be found here – at least we have something to go on. The man who found the Staffordshire Hoard didn't have a clue, it was pure luck. I think David's theory about a missing second hoard is well thought out.'

'Yes but I doubt we will find anything, it will all be a big disappointment,' said Jack, unkindly. He never liked it much when Lou bestowed praise on David. He had been the first of them to meet her of course – a chance encounter on the beach at Abersoch so he always saw her as being his friend first and foremost.

'Like we've said,' went on Lou, 'it doesn't matter if we find any treasure, does it? It's given us a second holiday which we never thought we'd have. So I think we should all raise our mugs of tea and say, three cheers to David!'

David blushed with pride. He felt pleased with himself. Clearly, it wouldn't matter if they didn't find anything, the important thing was he had got them together again for a nice holiday. David felt particularly chuffed that he had been so keen on coming camping. At the start of the summer holidays, before they had ever met Lou, he had been a real stay-at-home mummy's boy. Now, he was so different. In a week's time he would go back to school with his head held high, full of confidence. The playground bullies who used to torment him as a weak, bookish thing would find the old David had gone for good.

Part of him was itching to get moving with metal detector and shovel, yet like the others, he felt content merely to breathe in the sights and sounds of their new surroundings. The conversation between them flagged somewhat as they sat contentedly on their logs, feeling very grown up and independent.

'Oh, I've just thought,' said Jack, suddenly. 'We ought to phone home to let mum and dad know we've got here safely. They'll be wondering how we're getting on.'

'Good idea,' said Lou. 'I sent my folks a text to say I'm here about an hour ago. They haven't bothered to reply to it,' she added dryly.

The others looked at Lou sympathetically. It wasn't fair that she should have such neglectful parents – her mother in particular was a most unpleasant character whom Lou had little time for. Her father was agreeable enough but usually too busy as a freelance journalist to spend much time with her.

Jack dug out his mobile phone buried deep into a rucksack pocket. There were four missed calls already! Their mum had been trying to get hold of them but he hadn't heard his phone ring. He dialled home quickly, anxious to make amends. He couldn't get through – the phone was busy. He would have to ring later.

'Another thing that's simply great about this holiday,' said Emily, a few minutes later, lying lazily on her back in the dry grass, head propped up on her rucksack as a makeshift pillow, 'is that there is not a baddy in sight. We can go out treasure hunting without having to dodge smugglers or any other strange people for that matter.'

'Very true,' said Jack, who was trying again to get through to his mum and dad, but without success.

'Most probably she's on the phone to one of the boffins in the history society,' said David. 'Those lot can talk for England once they get going.'

~~~~~

David was almost right. His mother *was* on the phone to a history boffin – although he wasn't actually a member of their society.

'Oh it's lovely to hear from you Malcolm,' said his mother, cradling the phone in her shoulder as she stirred a pan on the kitchen stove. 'I am so looking forward to your forthcoming talk at our next meeting – we all are. There has been great interest in our society in the Staffordshire Hoard and it will be good to have a real expert on the Anglo-Saxon era along to talk about it.

'In fact the whole thing has been on my mind these last couple of days. My own children have become gripped by the story – you know what the young imagination is like. If I tell you that they have gone tearing off to Staffordshire in search of an undiscovered second hoard would you believe it?'

'Really?,' replied Dr Malcolm Finchfield, antique dealer and historian. 'Well I never, whatever gave them that idea?'

'Oh some old, moth-eaten Victorian book on ancient antiquities that my son David fished out of the loft. It
~~~~~

belonged to my great-great grandfather who was something of an authority on these matters,' said Mrs Johnson. 'David found a passage in it which described the location of two hoards a few miles apart – one of which is approximately where the Staffordshire Hoard was eventually dug up, interestingly.

'So, kids being kids they've gone on a mad, wild-goose chase trying to find the other one. The book makes clear that neither site had yielded any such treasure despite centuries of folk looking for it.'

'Hmm, how interesting and yes, as you say, a mad idea, quite ludicrous,' replied Dr Finchfield. 'Mind you, it will be an exciting, if fruitless pursuit for them. I say, that book does sound rather intriguing, I'm fond of old books and particularly the theories of historians from the Victorian era. I don't suppose I might borrow it? It would be rather a novelty to refer to their perspective in the talk I'm to give.'

'Well of course, I'll post it to you shall I – and if you'll take care of it and be good enough to return it to me when you come over to Malpas?' said Mrs Johnson.

'Certainly,' said Dr Finchfield, pulling at his wispy grey moustache as he spoke, as he always did when extremely curious about something. 'I look forward to addressing your gathering, I hear you are quite a keen bunch of historians in Malpas!'

'Yes, some of us are keener than others,' replied Mrs Johnson. 'We always get a good turn-out for our meetings, it's getting folk to take responsibility for running the society and serving on the committee – that's the big challenge.'

'It's always the way I'm afraid,' replied Dr Finchfield. 'Always the hard-working few who have to run around after everyone else. Anyway, I won't keep you, Mrs Johnson. It was a pleasure to talk to you and I will see you in September at your next meeting. Oh and I look forward to having sight of that old book of your great-great grandfather's. I will look after it well.'

~~~~~

After two rounds of open-air tea the children were lying on their backs on the soft, green grass carpet of their campsite, looking up at the tops of the poplar trees. The swish-swish of the branches was lulling them towards sleep.

They couldn't feel safer and more relaxed. The thrill tinged with fear of being on their own was tempered with the knowledge that the farmer and his wife were kind souls and if they were in any difficulty, would be only too glad to help them.

They had five full days to enjoy the camping life and amble around with a metal detector, listening out for the magic beep which might signify long-forgotten riches in the ground below. They could cycle through country lanes and swim in a crystal-clear lake. They could cook their own meals on their stove. And when the shadows over the cornfields lengthened and darkness closed in, they could dive into their tents and snuggle up inside their sleeping bags, dreaming of what tomorrow might bring.

As the children's eyes closed and the sun sailed westwards in a clear sky, the shadows of the poplars lengthened over their new 'Staffordshire den' as Emily insisted on calling it.

Then suddenly, Jack's mobile phone burst into life. It was his mother ringing back.

'Hello mum,' said Jack, groggily. 'We must have fallen asleep. The fresh air has made us sleepy for some reason. I tried ringing you earlier but it was engaged. David reckoned you must have been on the phone to one of your history society friends.'

'Well David was right,' said his mum. 'There's a chap
~~~~~

who is an expert on local antiquities and he's going to come and give a talk on the Staffordshire Hoard at our next meeting. David might like to come along and meet him. We had a jolly interesting chat.'

'Oh good,' said Jack, cutting across his mother before she had a chance to launch into a long account of what some history expert had to say. 'Anyway we are safely installed in our tree-lined campsite in a field in the middle of nowhere. It's right out in the countryside round here, you'd love it. The farmer and his wife are nice. Their daughter seems a bit odd but we shouldn't see too much of her hopefully.'

'She's probably not used to people coming to camp,' said Mrs Johnson. 'Anyway, I'm glad you're settling in well, I was a little worried about you, especially after your escapades at Abersoch and Whistling Sands.'

'Well have no fear, mum, this time it will be different. Not a smuggler in sight around here. We shall just spend our time walking, cycling and treasure hunting.'

'It sounds lovely, wish I was a child again and could spend my days doing those things. Now you will remember to eat properly won't you – the farm can provide you with basics and there's a shop in the village.'

'We know all that, mum, because it was we who found it out remember – or rather Lou did. You've got to remember we're a lot more independent now and able to stand on our own two feet.'

His mother laughed. 'That's good to know,' she said. 'I hope you have a wonderful time and I shall expect you to call me every day, or at least send a text message to let me and your father know that you're ok.'

Jack promised and said goodbye, feeling ever so slightly strange as he ended the call. He glanced at the others slumped on the grass and felt a mixture of pride with a slight chill of disquiet at being away from home and his mum and dad. He was still only 12 after all, and he'd had a sheltered life. It was hard in a way, knowing he wouldn't see them for several days.

On the other hand it was fantastic to be with Lou again. He gazed fondly at her – he counted her as his best friend now, even if they lived too far away to meet up often. It was odd how much he enjoyed the company of David and Emily when they were together like this. There wasn't half so much bickering between them as when they were at home with mum and dad.

Lou stirred. 'Oh I can't believe I've fallen asleep – it's the country air on top of that huge breakfast.'

'Get that kettle boiling will you Jack, let's have another brew and then decide what to do with the rest of the day.'

Jack did as he was told and the sound of it bubbling on their stove roused David and Emily. Soon they were sitting up and nursing another hot mug of tea.

'I think it's too late to go metal detecting this afternoon,' decided Lou. 'It's pushing four o'clock now. Why don't we go for a walk around the fields and woodlands and take a look at that lake. It will give us some idea where we want to start with the metal detector.'

'Also we need to be careful we search in an organised way,' pointed out Jack, or we could find ourselves going over the same ground twice.

'Very true, said Lou, 'we ought to mark the ground into grids and draw up a map of the field which we can shade in to show that we've searched a particular part. I've brought a notepad and a few pens and pencils with me, in case it was useful.

The others didn't flag up that they hadn't thought of any such thing. They would be at a loss without someone like Lou.

'Come on,' said Lou, springing up. 'We've sat around enough today. Let's get moving and explore a bit.'

The four of them stepped out of the circle of trees and made their way to the gate at the top of the field. The farmer had left it ajar as there were no animals either side needing to be kept in. It was ploughed, as Mr Owen had said, but there was a wide grassy bank around its edges along which the children could easily walk. Unlike some farmers, Mr Owen had left uncultivated patches of land to encourage birds, butterflies and other wildlife. The bank was dotted with vivid flowers – pink campion, buttercups, hedge parsley, numerous dancing poppies, the occasional bright blue cornflower and several others whose names they didn't know.

'I wish I knew what these lovely flowers were called,' said Emily. 'Oh and is that honeysuckle I can smell?'

It was. Wild honeysuckle threaded its way among the hedgerow shrubs, filling the evening air with a sweet scent. The western border of the field bent inwards quite sharply and beyond the hedge, the children glimpsed the occasional sparkle in the late afternoon sunshine.

'Oh I bet that's the lake,' said Emily. 'Let's go and see.'

As they approached, they could see a glimmer of it through the tree branches which surrounded it. David felt his heart beating faster. They were approaching the area where Anglo-Saxon treasure was supposed to have been buried, all those centuries ago.

He looked across at the neat tractor furrows left in the ploughed soil and trembled at the thought that something historic and valuable might lie beneath that ordinary-looking earth, just waiting for someone to dig it up.

The others had already run ahead through the trees and were whooping with delight at the sight of the hidden lake. There, in the centre, was the tiny island of trees, as described in the old Victorian book. Without doubt, they had come to the place where it was once believed that treasure was hidden.

The water of the lake was clear, appearing yellow-brown at first sight only because that was the colour of the bed itself. Long, elegant bulrushes and reeds hung over the water's edge. To Emily's delight, an inquisitive blue dragonfly flew up almost into her face before speeding off.

'Oh this is a lovely place, we could bathe in this water and swim in it, surely?' she asked Lou.

'The farmer said we could and I'm sure he's right. It looks absolutely pure,' said Lou. 'We shall have to bring our swimming gear tomorrow and jump in to cool off after a long day's metal detecting.'

The children walked around the lake two or three times and then headed back to their own field and their campsite in the trees. The fresh air, exercise and excitement was making them deliciously sleepy – but hungry too.

They feasted on tinned ravioli and crusty bread, washed down with ice cold stream water and some fruit for dessert and then decided to turn in for the night – Lou and Emily in one tent and the boys in the other.

The four of them were determined not to sleep straight-away. They wanted to savour the bliss of being in a sleeping bag, under canvas out in the countryside. They could hear the leaves of the tall poplar trees whispering and rustling. By the time bright stars pricked the sky and an owl began to hoot they were sound asleep.

CHAPTER FIVE

Treasure hunt begins

THE following day, Lou awoke first. That was no surprise, she had always been an early riser. She slipped on some clothes and stepped out of the tent and through the circle of trees.

The sky in the east was pink and grey, streaked with yellow. The sun was about to rise above the hills but hadn't done so yet. Without needing to look at her watch, she knew that it must be around 6am. Half a dozen clangs of the church bell confirmed that. She leaned against a tree and watched wistfully as the golden orb of the sun appeared, sending forth warm beams of light and making the spire and weather vane on the village church shine.

It was sure to be another nice day and pretty hot too, she guessed. They would do well to make an early start with the metal detector. It might become quite onerous, heavy-going work with the midday sun beating down. The best way to rouse the others, she concluded, was with the smell of bacon and tomatoes sizzling in the pan. If that didn't do it, nothing would.

Sure enough, before long the others were scrambling out through the tent flaps.

'Mmm that smells delicious,' said Jack, still inside his sleeping bag. 'Have you been up long Lou, did we over-sleep?'

'No, not at all, but I want us to get going with the metal detector early while it's still fairly cool. We can always come back here and have a nap later on when it's gets hot.'

'Doesn't food taste wonderful out of doors?' said Emily, as she sunk her teeth into a bacon and tomato butty, drizzled with brown sauce. One of the characters in the book she was reading had said exactly the same thing. It was absolutely true. The others nodded in agreement, their mouths too full to actually say anything.

After two rounds of tea, with the time approaching seven o'clock, the four children set out towards the adjacent field. Jack had put some refreshing lemonade and some snacks into a rucksack which he slung over his shoulders. Lou carried her dad's metal detector and headphones under her arm. Under David's arm were the two big spades the farmer had lent them. Lou had a notepad and pencil in her jeans pocket to mark the area they were to search.

They were immensely excited because it occurred to them that even if no Anglo-Saxon treasure was to be found, they might still uncover other valuable and historic objects from centuries past.

'This area here is to the east of the lake,' said Lou, pointing. 'It's easy to tell since the sun is still firmly in the east. What's not so easy is to say where exactly the treasure site might be. There is a lot of field to the east and we are going to have to be careful how we search it.'

'Lou, can you see how there appear to be pairs of regular horizontal lines gouged into the soil by the plough?' pointed out David. 'They appear to run from the lake across to the field border on the other side. Well if you look, they seem to be dividing up the field into more or less equal segments.'

'Yes you're right,' said Lou. 'Well spotted, David. That means we could start at the top and work our way down, one segment at a time, making sure that we cover all the land in each one. Let's go to the top of the field now and count each segment and then I'll mark them up on my home-made map.'

The four of them slowly walked the field from top to bottom, keeping their eyes rooted on the two deep, horizontal grooves in the soil left by the plough at regular intervals across the field. By the time they got to the seventh they were beyond the southern end of the lake. If the old book was to be believed, that was the furthest south they would need to scour with the metal detector.

Lou crouched and began marking the segments on her map, as accurately as she could. She numbered them from one to seven.

'Now we need to go back to the top of the field and start with segment one,' said Lou.

It took her a few minutes to sort out the metal detector and work out the best setting to have it on. She put the headphones on and tested it by waving it above the metal spades. It emitted a loud and steady beep.

'Ouch,' cried Lou, 'where's the volume control on this thing? Well, the equipment works, that's for sure! Ok everyone? Now I propose David starts off with the metal detector since all this was his idea. When his arms start to feel like dropping off, Jack and I will have a turn. Emily, I'm not sure you're quite strong enough – these things aren't light.'

'That's ok,' said Emily, who rarely minded taking a back seat with such things. She was content enough to be there and pleased that the holiday was proceeding safely and proving to be interesting rather than exciting.

David put the headphones on and took the metal detector from Lou bursting with excitement. His arms were trembling so much he barely needed to swish the thing. Lou watched him rather impatiently.

'David you're going to risk missing something interesting if you don't use it properly. Keep the thing steady and close to the ground and sweep carefully from side to side and walk in a straight line.'

Lou put up with David's less than competent performance until he got to the field boundary on the far side. Somewhat disappointed, David handed the metal detector over to her. The thing hadn't beeped once – not even with a false alarm! Never mind, there was plenty of field left for them to search.

Lou more or less retraced David's steps since she was convinced he wasn't doing it properly. Somewhat to his embarrassment within a few yards, she heard a loud beep through the headphones!

'I think I may have something!' she exclaimed in excitement. 'Come on, give me a spade, David, and I'll take a good look.'

Fortunately, the soil was well tilled and the spade cut into it easily. It had rained heavily in Staffordshire the previous week and although the earth was dry enough to walk on, underneath it was still damp. The sharp edge had no trouble sinking deep into the ground. What would it bring up? The others crowded round.

Lou dug up a couple of spadefuls when she hit upon something distinctly metallic.

'Here,' said Emily, 'I brought the trowel, I thought it might be useful.'

It was. Lou took it gratefully and carefully levered up the metal object. It wasn't so big when the earth had been scraped off. It was in fact an antique coat button, almost certainly a century and more old.

They looked at it with interest. It had little or no value of course, but it occurred to them that they were the first people in over 100 years to see that thing, and to hold it in their hands. Who dropped it, they wondered, so long ago? Who wore that coat and how did it come to lie there, in that particular field?

'I'll keep this,' said Lou. 'I feel it is a good omen and maybe a sign of better things to come.'

'You'll keep what?' came the harsh, sneering voice of a girl behind them.

The four children span round. It was Becky, the farmer's daughter, who had sneaked up without them noticing. Lou could have kicked herself – she was normally exceptionally good at sensing the presence of others around her, particularly those she distrusted.

'I thought you promised to share everything you found with my parents? You'll do no such thing of course, you'll keep it for yourselves. You're little better than thieves,' snarled Becky.

'Hey, don't you speak to us like that, you rude girl, you don't know what you're talking about,' snapped Jack who had taken an instant dislike to Becky the previous day.

'It's a button, Becky, an old coat button which isn't worth a penny. I simply wanted to keep it as a curiosity that's all,' replied Lou, calmly. 'Here, you have it if you like.'

Becky looked in disgust at the muddy disc in Lou's palm.

'Oh fine, you give us the worthless trinkets while you keep the valuable stuff,' replied Becky, unimpressed. 'I don't like you lot and I don't trust you and I don't see why we should have you invading our lovely farmland.'

'We haven't found any valuable stuff, as you put it,' replied Lou, again calmly and coolly. 'We quite possibly never will.'

Lou could unleash a furious temper when she wanted to, but was not willing to waste such energy on Becky. In any case, she still intended to find out who this uncouth, unpleasant girl really was, beneath the unpleasant bravado. Was she as bad as she seemed?

'Why don't you come and join us for an hour or so and help us look,' said Lou. 'Have you ever used a metal detector before? You might find it fun.'

Becky curled her lip in disgust at Lou and flicked back her tumbling long hair disdainfully.

'You don't fool me,' she said. 'I know your sort and believe me, I'll be watching you like a hawk while you're here. Don't think you're going to make off with valuables from this farm without anyone knowing.'

'Are you worried, Becky,' said Lou, in that hypnotising voice of hers, her vivid eyes locked hard onto hers. Lou walked right up to her. 'Are you worried about this place, are your parents struggling to make it pay? I know how difficult farming can be these days.'

'What would you know about farming?' retorted Becky. 'Do you live on a farm? You have no idea what a hard life it is or what long hours farmers must work.'

'I live in the country just like here,' said Lou, quietly, 'although I don't have a biggish town three miles away like you, we are a long way from anywhere. I know plenty of farmers all around me, and life is tough for them right now. Don't hate us for being here, our parents are paying your parents for our accommodation and any food your mum gives us. Surely that's useful income?'

Just for a fleeting second, Becky's hostile demeanour appeared to soften. Then Jack, with less than perfect timing, made the row flare up again.

'Perhaps if you did more around the farm to help your parents, instead of sulking and being a pain, life wouldn't be such a struggle,' he said to her. 'I mean, you don't exactly dress for farm work, do you?'

Jack had a good point, although it was a pity he had felt the need to make it. Becky certainly didn't dress to be of any practical use around the farm. Her boots were fashionable brushed suede, hardly the sort you'd want to wear traipsing through cow sheds. Her clothes were smart and she wore jewellery like a grown-up.

But she was furious with Jack's assessment of her. Becky turned a cold, withering gaze upon him. Jack began to tremble visibly.

'Who asked you, you pathetic worm,' she screeched. 'I'll have you know I do help around this farm. I know how to milk cows, I know how to feed sheep, I have spent hours driving the tractor up and down ploughing and moving and stacking hay bales. Just because I don't dress like a tramp like you!

'Now you keep out of my way or I'll come after you in the tractor.'

Then, revoltingly, Becky spat at Jack before turning and stomping off towards the farmhouse. Fortunately, her mouthful of spittle fell short.

Lou gripped the spade handle so tightly, her knuckles turned white.

'I feel like coshing her over the head with this thing,' she said. 'Only then we'd get sent home, and she would have won. Take no notice of her Jack, she's vile and she'll come a cropper one day.'

Jack looked deflated and dejected. He had been feeling more and more self-confident recently, but Becky's insults had burst him like a balloon. No-one had ever spat at him before.

'I think you're great,' said Lou, rubbing his shoulder.

'We all do,' said Emily, giving her brother a rare hug. She realised how upset he was. 'Let's not allow that horrible girl to spoil our fun, she's nothing to us.'

'Maybe she's right, maybe we are just treasure hunters, seeking to make off with hidden wealth which should belong to her parents,' said Jack slowly, looking about him.

'They will get half of anything of value that we find,' said Lou, 'which at the moment is precisely half of nothing. Look, if by a miracle we do find what we are looking for, we could always give up any right to keep our share and let them have the lot. I'm not interested in trying to become rich and I know what it's like to have parents who are hard up, I would hate to think that Mr and Mrs Owen might have to sell their wonderful farm because they can't pay the bills.'

The four of them agreed and felt much better for it. For them, searching for treasure was the fun bit, not keeping it, or claiming a huge reward. Whatever they found they would willingly renounce any right to, in order that such a hard-working, decent farming couple like Mr and Mrs Owen could have the extra cash they greatly needed.

'Come on,' said Lou. 'We're not getting very far down this field. Let's keep searching and then, when we're tired and fed up, we'll throw ourselves into that wonderful lake and swim until we're shiny and clean.'

The others chuckled. It wasn't easy to feel down at heart for long with someone like Lou around. They kept going with the metal detector, taking regular turns. Even Emily had a go, although it was too heavy for her. She was after all, still only 10.

They were half way through the third segment of the field with Jack having taken over the detector when he gave a cry. A distinct beep! Jack swished over the spot two or three times to be certain where it was coming from. Lou handed him the spade and he began to dig down.

At first it looked like another coat button. Jack carefully brushed the mud off it and as he did so, saw a glint of silver. It was an old shilling! Jack had seen such coins lying around at home. They had, after all, been in circulation when his parents were growing up but this appeared to be much older than any of them.

'Oh Jack, look at the date on it!' said Lou, squeezing his arm. 'Oh you clever thing – this is a shilling from 1787 and look at the engraving of the king on the back of it – Georgius III Dei Gratia'.

'That means George III by the Grace of God,' chipped in David, looking on rather jealously.

'This is a real piece of history! That coin was dropped in this field in 1787 and you are the first person to touch it since then,' enthused Lou, determined to cheer Jack up.

'Well not necessarily,' David couldn't resist adding. 'It was minted in 1787 in the reign of King George III but it might have been dropped, say, 10 years later – or yesterday for that matter.'

'Of course it wasn't dropped yesterday, David, just because you haven't found anything valuable yet, there's no need to sulk,' said Lou, impatiently. 'This will definitely be worth something. Ok, it's not an ancient artefact but it's still a great find and something to be proud of!'

Jack looked up and grinned, and then back at the coin in his hand. It was the most surreal and rewarding experience to discover something like that lying a few inches below the surface of a farmer's field. He glanced about him, wondering what the place would have looked like back in the late 1700s when George III was on the throne. Who last held that coin in his hand? How Jack would have loved to know.

'Would this be a good point to take a break and go off and have our swim, especially as it is getting rather hot now?' suggested Lou. 'Also we do need to get to the shops this afternoon or our campfire feasts will start becoming rather poor affairs.'

The others agreed. Metal detecting was actually quite tiring, time-consuming work. It had been great fun, despite the appearance of Becky, but a swim in that lake seemed ever more appealing as the sun climbed higher. Emily definitely wanted to go off shopping later that afternoon and see more of the quaint and interesting village of Wall.

As they headed over to the lake, Lou's cat-like eyes darted in all directions, looking out for Becky. She was nowhere to be seen – so much the better. Lou still couldn't decide for sure whether she was a bad egg. She possibly might not be, despite her loutish behaviour earlier. One thing was certain: that girl was not to be trusted. They would have to be careful from now on and keep an eye out for her.

What a pity that the danger of smugglers on their holiday in North Wales had been replaced by a pointless, stupid threat from a silly, spiteful girl like Becky.

Such concerns were forgotten by the time the four of them had changed into their swimming trunks and costumes and plunged into the clear water of the lake. It was delightfully warm in the shallow part, but colder as they swam towards the centre where it was too deep to stand up.

'Who would have thought it, our own private swimming pool!' laughed Emily as she dived beneath the surface.

The four of them swam and splashed about until they were tired and hungry. There were two useful hours left of the day and it was time to get to the village and stock up. They felt fresh, clean and glowing as they walked back to their campsite.

They had eaten nothing since breakfast save for a couple of snacks while metal-detecting. Lou recalled seeing a café in the village and they decided, as a treat, to call there for a drink and a bite to eat. That would keep them going until their evening meal.

The village of Wall was an intriguing place with leafy lanes bordered with nicely kept hedges and ivy-clad walls. Big, expensive-looking houses sat at the end of long gravel drives. Yet it still felt rural. Cows mooed in the surrounding fields and sheep baaed. It was much like Lou's part of Shropshire.

The café was sturdy and old-fashioned, built from red, weather-beaten brick with arched window frames and small leaded panes of glass. A stripy canopy hung over wooden tables and chairs in the street below.

'Oh let's sit outside,' said Emily, 'and watch the world go by. I haven't been to a café as nice as this since the one we went to in Aberdaron, do you remember?'

The others nodded – they called in there while hot on the trail of smugglers. How could they forget! Nothing quite so exciting was in prospect this time, of course.

The children sat contentedly munching some delicious jam and cream scones, which slipped down excellently with glasses of ice-cold lemonade. It was what they needed. The conversation flagged as the four of them simply enjoyed gazing out on the cobbled square.

The village shop was opposite. Its front door opened and out came a familiar couple – it was the farmer and his wife, Mr and Mrs Owen. Emily, who had been glancing across at the shop trying to decide what they should buy for supper, noticed them first. She gave them a friendly wave. The couple came over for a chat.

'Well, this is very civilised,' said Mrs Owen. 'Those scones look delicious, I've a good mind to drag my husband in and get some.'

'Oh no, we've spent enough today as it is,' replied Mr Owen with a grin.

'Mr Owen, we were thinking,' said Emily, looking at Lou and the others as she spoke. 'We have decided . . .' She faltered, feeling it best that it come from Lou.

'What Emily's trying to say,' said Lou, 'is that if we dig up anything of value with our metal-detecting – we want you both to have the full reward from it. We don't think it's fair we have anything. We know how hard it must be, running a farm these days.'

The couple beamed at them and looked at each other, a little embarrassed.

'Now listen,' said Mr Owen. 'It's sweet of you but anything you dig up we will share as finders and landowners. That's the way it's always been done and it's good enough for us. We want you to have a good time with us and enjoy yourselves. You're right, life is tough but that's for grown-ups to worry about. At your age, carry on doing what you're doing – exploring and finding out about the world. I wish our Becky had as much spirit as the four of you.'

‘Please tell her, she’s welcome to spend some time with us, if she’d like to,’ said Lou. ‘We’d like to get to know her.’

‘That’s brave of you!’ said Mrs Owen, looking pleased nonetheless. ‘Well talking of Becky, we better get back to the farm, to make sure she’s not up to any mischief. Do call in later if you want some more supplies.’

CHAPTER SIX

Becky deals a spiteful blow

A BORED-LOOKING Becky was sprawled out on the sofa in the roomy living room. She liked having the place to herself with no-one around nagging her to do this and do that.

The welcome peace and quiet was broken by the shrill peal of the telephone. The bell was loud and would ring outside in the farmyard as well. Becky was determined not to answer it. She hated being sucked into long conversations with some nosy relative demanding to know her business. Usually if she ignored it, the caller would be content merely to leave a message.

That day, the phone kept ringing and ringing. It would stop, but five to 10 minutes later, it would ring again. It was no good, she would have to get up and answer it the next time. It wasn't long before it rang yet again. Becky dragged herself from the sofa and picked up the receiver. Putting on her frostiest telephone voice, she answered, 'hello, Home Farm?'

'Oh good afternoon to you,' replied a cultured male voice. 'I hope I haven't called at an inconvenient moment. I realise how busy you must be.'

'My parents aren't in,' replied Becky, coldly. 'Can I take a message?'

'Well,' replied the well-spoken gentleman, 'you can indeed. In fact you may even be able to assist me yourself.'

Becky rolled her eyes and squeezed the receiver, as if it was the caller's neck. Who was this annoying man, disturbing her afternoon?

'I'll try,' she said, forcing herself to sound polite.

'Well my dear,' said the gentleman. 'I am anxious to find a place to stay in your picturesque parish and I was particularly hoping I might pitch a tent on your campsite. I believe I am right in thinking that your farm allows camping? I am terribly keen on exploring your delightful part of the world and being at one with nature. I cannot think of a better way to do so than under canvas.'

Becky was about to retort that they most certainly did not usually take campers, when a mischievous idea crossed her mind. What better way to infuriate those kids playing at being grown up and fending for themselves, than if some kindly, elderly man ended up pitching his tent a few yards away? With livestock scattered about, there was only one field where camping was suitable. What a shock it would be to find some silver-haired old fuddy-duddy invading their space!

'Yes indeed, my parents welcome campers,' she replied. 'When would you like to book in?'

'Oh as soon as possible I think, no time like the present! What say I come over tomorrow morning and you can show me where I can put up my little canvas palace. Tell me young lady, are there any other campers on site?'

'Yes, there is a party of four youngsters, two boys and two girls, who are staying in tents in a circle of trees in the camping field. They're on their own without their parents so perhaps you could check on them from time to time and make sure they're ok?'

'Oh I would be delighted,' he replied. 'I'm sure we'll get on famously. Now, I must give you my name: it's Fitzgerald, Mr Andrew Fitzgerald. I look forward to meeting you and your parents tomorrow – and indeed the young campers!'

'See you tomorrow then, Mr Fitzgerald,' replied Becky, a sly grin crossing her face.

'Hah!' she cried doing a jig across the living room floor and clapping her hands. That was one phone call well worth taking. The treasure hunters would be furious – especially if that nice old man kept checking up on them. He sounded the sort who would, that's for sure.

~~~~~

Becky was still wearing a silly grin when her parents got home half an hour later.

'You seem to be in a good mood, unusual for you,' Mrs Owen said to her daughter. 'Here, make yourself useful, help me with some of these shopping bags.'

Becky, feeling cheerful for a change, did as she was asked.

'I was making myself useful while you were out, for your information,' crowed Becky, her face lit up with malevolent pleasure.

'Really?' said her dad. 'I take it you weren't hosing down the cow sheds or laying fresh straw in the barns, judging by the pristine state of your clothes.'

'No dad, I was helping you diversify – I think that's what it's called,' replied Becky. 'I've managed to get you another happy camper who is coming tomorrow and keen to stay for a few days. That will be some more useful income for you. Isn't that brilliant?'

Mr and Mrs Owen looked at each other, perplexed. They really hadn't had any intention of taking in holidaymakers, although the extra money would be welcome. They had allowed Lou and the Johnson children to camp more as a favour than anything else, not wishing to discourage youngsters keen to explore.

When Becky told them that it was an elderly man with a passion for birdlife and the countryside, they were cross. It wasn't that they had any problem with that sort of person in principle, but they knew that Lou and the others prized their independence, away from grown-ups for a bit. They would hate having their space invaded in that way.
~~~~~

'I know when you wear that silly, smug face of yours,' said her mother. 'You put on that particular expression when you feel you've got one over on people. You have taken a totally irrational dislike to those lovely children and you have arranged for some well-meaning old duffer to pitch up close by knowing that would get on their nerves. You're a mean girl, I don't where you get it from.'

'Oh mum I don't know why the pair of you are so keen on those kids,' said Becky. 'They're a bunch of treasure hunters hoping to whisk away anything valuable they find on our land and make their fortunes with it.'

'Now it's funny you should say that, Becky, because we have just met "those kids" in the village, having tea and scones at the café,' said her father, frowning at her. 'They actually offered to give anything they find to us – the whole lot. We refused and said they had every right to a half share. They most probably won't find anything of value but that shows you how decent they are. It's a pity you have to judge everybody else by your own low standards.

'Now if you took a telephone number for that fellow, we will ring him back and tell him politely that we are fully booked and he can stay next week if he wishes.'

Becky hadn't taken a number for him, of course, and their telephone had not logged his number either. There was no way of stopping him turning up the following morning and no choice but to let him camp in the same field as the others. At least they were encircled by trees, but nonetheless, they would be certain to feel put-out.

Becky looked sheepish to hear that the four of them had offered to hand anything they found over to her parents.

'You've only got their word for that, of course,' she said. 'Most probably they'll snaffle stuff away in their rucksacks and you won't be any the wiser. If there's some nosey old git helping keep tabs on them, then that's a good thing, if you ask me.'

'Becky, no-one is asking you anything right now, believe me,' replied her mother, 'unless it be to shut up. You are a thorough nuisance and you have been throughout the summer holidays. I don't know what's got into you. You're lonely but you won't go anywhere or meet any of your school friends. You won't come shopping with me to Lichfield. You've got no interest in life and for a girl of 14 that's not a good thing.'

Becky decided not to stick around to listen to any more and stormed off to her bedroom. She lay on her bed and kicked at the collection of cuddly toys sitting in a row at the foot of her duvet, sending them scattering. What was it about parents that they had to be so annoying and patronising? Why couldn't they leave her alone? She was on a six-week summer holiday, if she wanted to stroll around doing nothing, then she would do nothing. What did they expect her to do, put on overalls every day and muck out the pigsty, or go round the village sweeping chimneys?

She had done them a favour agreeing to let that boring old man come to stay, it would bring them in money they badly needed. If it got on the nerves of those children who had turned up from nowhere, pretending to be grown-ups, then so much the better. Becky wasn't finished with them either. She'd keep a close watch, especially on that tough-looking girl with the sharp green eyes.

Anyhow, let's see what tomorrow brings, she thought, when their silver-haired guardian turns up. Becky smiled another of her sly smiles, pushed her face into her pillow and, even though it was only late afternoon, drifted into sleep.

~~~~~

As Becky dozed, Lou, Jack, David and Emily were staggering back across the now familiar farmland bound
~~~~~

for their tree-lined campsite. They had bought plenty of supplies from the village shop and were struggling to carry it all.

Fortunately, Lou had had the foresight to take her rucksack but the rest of the shopping was in carrier bags with thin handles which cut into their fingers as they walked.

'Oh I wish that sun would go away for a bit,' groaned David. 'I'm getting so hot weighed down with all this stuff. Can't we borrow one of Mr Owen's donkeys or something and load the beast up with big panniers?'

'You're the donkey,' said Lou, chuckling. 'You know perfectly well modern farms don't use donkeys like that any more. Your trouble David is that you're still not as fit as you should be. I think you've put on a couple of pounds since we were at Abersoch. We'll have to march you around a bit more and get you some regular exercise.'

'He's had his head back in his books, Lou,' said Jack, who was also sweating under the weight of his heavy load. 'He's moved on from Teach Yourself Welsh to teach yourself ancient history from centuries-old books.'

David scowled at both of them but said nothing – he was too out of breath for an argument.

'Well David shouldn't be mocked for his love of books,' pointed out Lou. 'I love books too, and old ones can be fascinating. That's a point David, I don't suppose you brought that old Victorian one on antiquities of your mum's – the one which suggested a hoard of Anglo-Saxon treasure near that lake?'

David shook his head. It would have been far too heavy to carry, of course.

'Why do you ask,' he said.

'Oh no reason,' replied Lou. 'I suppose it's perfectly safe at your parents' place and isn't likely to be seen by anyone else?'

'I doubt it would be,' said David. 'I think I was about the first person in a century to so much as hold it in my hands and open it.'

They slipped through the poplar trees and out of the direct sunlight with relief. It was no fun walking in such heat trying to carry all that shopping. They flopped in the cool grass like panting dogs.

'Whose turn is it to get the kettle boiling and sort out the evening meal?' asked Lou, 'I don't see why it should always be me just 'cos I brought the stove.'

Emily smiled. 'I would love to rustle us up something tonight if that's ok,' she said. 'How about chicken casserole – I think I can manage it on that stove.'

'Oh Emily, that sounds great,' said Lou. 'What could be better? A cup of tea, then read a good book with the aroma of a chicken casserole rising into the country air! After that, I suggest we get an early night and get back out first thing tomorrow morning with the metal detector while it's cool, like we did this morning. Even earlier if we can manage it – we've still got more than half of that field to search.'

Emily's chicken casserole proved a remarkable success. Her brothers could hardly believe such a tasty meal could be prepared in such basic circumstances. Lou had to concede that she was quite possibly her equal in cooking if not better.

They went to bed early that night, tummies full of excellent food and minds buzzing with the events of their first full day of camping and the one to come.

'What I love about it, and what is making it such a real adventure for me,' enthused Emily to Lou as the pair of them snuggled into their sleeping bags, 'is that we are so entirely alone with not an adult in sight. It's great having this whole field to ourselves. At first I was a bit scared but I'm not any more.'

'Well it's like Mrs Owen told me when I rang up,' said Lou, 'they don't usually take campers but they took us as a favour because they wanted to let us have our fun, and plenty of fun it is proving to be.'

'Except for the run-ins with their horrible daughter Becky,' pointed out Emily.

'Oh don't let her worry you,' said Lou, 'I'm certainly not worried about her at all. She wants nothing to do with us which suits us fine. I doubt we shall see anything of her for the rest of our stay here. We only have to see the farmer and his wife when we want to and speak to our parents on the phone when we feel like it. Apart from that we are gloriously alone!'

CHAPTER SEVEN

A very unwelcome camper

THEY slept deeply. It was odd how comfortable you can be in a tent and how well you can sleep. Fresh air and exercise more than made up for the lack of a proper mattress. When they did stir, at around 5.15am when a cockerel heralded the start of a new day with a raucous cock-a-doodle-doo, the children felt refreshed and ready to get up.

'At home, I never feel like getting out of bed and when I do I'm all groggy,' said Jack, sitting up in their tent. Here I feel like springing up straightaway and getting moving.'

'Go and get the kettle on then,' mumbled David, yawning. He still liked to wake up gently, even if they were on a camping holiday.

Jack scrambled his way out of the tent. Lou had beaten him to it. The kettle was already on and beginning to bubble.

'I've been to the stream for a wash and to fill our water container,' she said, smiling at Jack. 'Hey, we're going to have a fantastic breakfast this morning – have you seen what Emily brought back from the shop? No wonder those bags were heavy yesterday.'

Jack peeked into the shopping bag which Emily had pushed under the flysheet of the girls' tent to keep cool – there were a couple of delicious-looking packs of smoked bacon, some big fat pork and leek sausages which Mrs Owen had given them, eggs from the farm's own hens and some appetising black pudding.

'Oh Lou, this looks fantastic. I'm so pleased we're here you know, back together and having such fun. I was getting bored stiff walking round the house, nothing to do,' said Jack.

Lou smiled. 'You see how different your life is now you've met me?' she told him. It wasn't a modest thing to say, but true, nonetheless.

Before long, the four of them – Emily and David still in their sleeping bags – were sitting on the tree stumps tucking into an almightily good English breakfast. By six o'clock, with the sun still not quite above the horizon, they set out again for another metal-detecting session.

'Right,' said Lou, as they strolled towards the top of the field. 'Now we had a valiant go yesterday, but in fact, we have still only done two of these horizontal bands marked by the blades of the plough. I've shaded them off here – we have at least another five to do to cover the area of the field to the east of the lake.

'We've made an early start this morning, so we should be able to have a good crack at it. We'll take it in turns with the metal detector as we did yesterday. I'll start us off. We'll do a couple of hours and then take a break for a coffee from the flask I've made up, or there's some lemonade.'

'Oh and I've brought some chocolate with us,' said Emily.

'Fine, let's get treasure hunting!' said Lou.

A couple of hours passed and the youngsters were making good progress but had little to show for their efforts. There had been a couple of false alarms followed by some feverish spadework. All they unearthed were bits of fence wire and a rusty old cartwheel, still with some wooden spokes radiating from its hub.

'They don't make 'em like that any more,' grinned Lou. 'I wonder when that wheel was last used on this farm – probably over a century ago. We ought to give that to Mr Owen, it quite possibly belonged to his great-grandfather or a generation further back. This farm has been in their family for 200 years, so Mrs Owen told me.'

David picked up the wheel and gazed at it, imagining it beneath an old farm cart, pulled by a horse in the days before tractors existed.

'Come on dreamer,' said Lou, 'I'm sure this land has more secrets to give up, I can sense it somehow.'

Emily glanced at Lou. Often, when Lou said such things, they had an uncanny habit of coming true.

They kept on for another half an hour. It was pushing nine o'clock and time for a break. They walked over to the grass verge and plonked themselves down.

'Let's not be too disappointed,' said Jack, realising that David appeared a trifle glum. 'We never really thought we would find any Anglo-Saxon treasure. Our reward is to be here and have this lovely countryside to ourselves.'

'Hang on, not quite to ourselves,' said Lou, glancing towards the gate at the bottom of the field. 'Who's that chap plodding his way along the grass verge? I wasn't aware of any public footpath or right of way through here.'

'We'll get a chance to ask him in a minute,' said Jack, suspiciously, 'he looks like he's heading towards us.'

Sure enough, the man was walking steadily around the perimeter of the field and they were sitting right in his path. Lou looked nervously at the metal detector and spades left messily on the ground, marking the spot they had reached. He was bound to see them and wonder what they were up to. Yet he would no doubt prove harmless enough.

'Good morning to you,' he said in a kindly, cultured voice as he reached them. The man was well-dressed in a rather old-fashioned style – tweed trousers, jacket and waistcoat and small, half-moon glasses. He had silver sideburns disappearing beneath a tweed flat cap and a moustache of the same colour to match. It made him look around 70 but Lou guessed he was probably a few years younger. 'Are you enjoying the fresh air and countryside?'

The children nodded, not particularly anxious to be drawn into conversation.

'Yes, it's a nice day to be out, isn't it?' said the man, giving a small, forced smile through rather greasy-looking thin lips. 'Well I must say, it's good to make your acquaintance since I think we might be neighbours over the next few days.'

Lou, Jack, David and Emily looked at him, baffled. What did he mean?

'I'm a fellow camper,' he announced. 'I believe you've pitched your tents in the circle of trees in the field yonder. I've pitched mine about half way up towards the hedge on the same side. Not too close to be a pain, I hope, but near enough should you need anything. The farmer's daughter told me you were on your own when I rang up to book in and she was a tad worried about you. She asked if I wouldn't mind keeping an eye out for you and of course, I readily agreed.'

The four of them stared in dismay at the slightly eccentric man in his old-fashioned tweed, with his thin lips, grey teeth and watery smile. They didn't like the look of him. He was a genteel sort all right, the type who would not be out of place at a garden party or an upmarket restaurant. This wasn't an unshaven crook like they had encountered at Abersoch but nonetheless, he made them uneasy.

As for having him check up on them, they couldn't think of anything worse. Becky had done this on purpose out of spite. How could she have been so mean!

Eventually the man broke the awkward silence. 'Erm, I haven't given you my name, it's Mr Fitzgerald – Andrew Fitzgerald. He looked at them expectantly, but they were in no mood to share their names with him.

'What brings you to this part of the world camping?' asked Lou, a cold edge to her voice. Without quite knowing why, she felt instantly suspicious of "Mr Fitzgerald" and what he was doing there.

'No doubt for the same reason as you, my dear,' he replied. Then he added, rather hurriedly, 'because I have a love of the countryside and its natural beauty and this is an area I am keen to explore. It must be great fun for the four of you to be camping alone too, but quite tough also, I would imagine, without your parents to guide you. In their absence, I will be happy to be of service.'

'We do not need our parents to guide us,' replied Lou, frostily. 'We have come here to enjoy the countryside and fresh air on our own. We don't want any grown-up's help I can assure you, so please don't feel the need to look out for us, we would rather you didn't.'

This was impolite but Lou was feeling a rising disdain for the man which she was finding difficult to disguise.

'Oh please don't misunderstand,' said Mr Fitzgerald, giving one of his thin smiles, 'I was merely expressing a concern for your welfare, that was all. I see you are indulging in a spot of metal detecting,' he continued, glancing at their detector and spades lying in a heap in the field. 'It's a fascinating hobby. Have you found anything so far?'

'Nothing noteworthy. Anyway, we won't keep you Mr erm, Fitzgerald, from your walk. It's the perfect day for it,' added Lou, struggling to say something pleasant.

'Indeed it is, indeed it is,' he replied. 'Well good luck with your treasure hunting! Do let me know if I can help you with anything.'

Since no-one had anything good to say about 'Mr Fitzgerald' they waited in silence until his rather large ears were sufficiently far away to overhear their conversation.

'What do you make of him?,' whispered David.

'I should make nothing of him save for the fact that he

has chosen to come here and camp virtually on top of us and is showing an excessive interest in what we are doing here,' said Lou, slowly.

'You're a good judge of character Lou, is he a good egg or a bad egg?' asked Jack.

'Probably a bad egg,' said Lou. 'There's something odd and fake about him. That dratted Becky! It sounds like she took his phone call – I bet it was when we were out in Wall yesterday and Mr and Mrs Owen were out, too. Probably by the time her parents got back to the house she had already agreed for him to stay. It must have occurred to her that we would hate having him anywhere near so she's welcomed him with open arms. It was pure spite because she's taken a dislike to us.'

The others looked glumly at Lou.

'This holiday isn't going to be half so much fun now with him parked a few yards away,' said Jack.

'Perhaps it might not be so bad to have a grown up near, in case we got into trouble or something,' suggested Emily meekly.

The others glared at her scornfully – even David.

'Anyway, bickering about it isn't going to change anything,' said Lou. 'He's cleared off now on his walk so let's forget about him and carry on metal detecting. He has no idea what we're looking for and why – he'll think we're a few kids having a silly game of treasure hunt.'

They felt better when they got back to the task in hand. Nothing could be done about Mr Fitzgerald save to ignore him and pretend he didn't exist.

A light breeze had got up that day and it was refreshing after the day before, allowing them to progress faster. To their excitement, the detector buzzed loudly through the headphones on three occasions. They dug carefully each time with great eagerness. All they found was more rusting fence wire, an old metal ointment tube and an iron bar of some kind. It was disappointing.

Lou straightened up, her back hurt after so much effort. She glanced about her and her sharp eyes caught a distinct flash appearing to come from the hedge at the bottom of the field. Only some form of glass reflecting bright sunlight would cause such a dazzling burst of light. The others hadn't noticed.

'I'm worried someone is spying on us,' she whispered. 'Let's carry on as normal as if we're unaware and I'll keep watch out of the corner of my eye.'

The others did as they were told and Lou pretended to keep digging. There was another flash, as if a pair of binoculars were being held aloft and catching the sun every now and then. But the hedge was too thick for Lou to see for sure.

'I'm going to flush out whoever is hiding in that hedge by running full pelt to the bottom of the field and straight through the gate,' she said.

She dropped her spade and tore off. Lou was an amazingly quick and agile runner. If anyone was hiding behind that hedge, they wouldn't have time to disappear. The gate wasn't shut and Lou passed quickly through it.

Sure enough, there was Mr Fitzgerald with a pair of binoculars in his hands! He was still at the top of the adjoining field but appeared to be looking in the opposite direction.

She ran up and confronted him. 'Can I ask what you're doing with those binoculars?'

'Oh hello my dear, I didn't see you there,' replied Mr Fitzgerald. 'I am a keen birdwatcher you know, and am anxious to get a better view of some of our wonderful feathered friends in the hedges and treetops around here. For instance, look at those lovely gold tits in that hawthorn bush over there with their wonderful red and yellow plumage, quite extraordinary.'

'They're goldfinches and that's a mountain ash, not a hawthorn,' Lou corrected him. 'Goldfinches are quite common in the countryside. I must get back to the others.'

'Aah, I stand corrected. Goodbye my dear,' replied Mr Fitzgerald, smiling again although his grey eyes looked small and cold. 'Good luck with your treasure hunting – have you found anything yet?'

Lou didn't reply and sped back to the others.

'Come on,' she said. 'Let's get back to the camp. I haven't got the heart to carry on metal detecting right now.'

'What's happened Lou? Was anyone there?' asked Emily, her blue opening wide.

'I'll tell you when we're back at the camp. I think we need to talk things through.'

They returned disconsolately, only to notice with horror that Mr Fitzgerald had put up a large red tent half-way up the field – almost within earshot if they were to talk reasonably loudly.

'Just look at what that selfish pig has done!' exclaimed David.

In truth, sharing the field with a real pig would have been a far more palatable option. If they had no real right to complain about another camper joining them in the field, why did he need to pitch his tent so close? Why not go for the opposite end so he and they had plenty of space?

'There's something strange about all this,' said Lou. 'Come on, let's not stand here staring, he's most probably watching right now. At least we've got trees all around us. Let's get some lunch on and have a talk.'

As their stove roared into life, Lou told them how she had seen Mr Fitzgerald seemingly scurrying away after she dashed through the gate.

'He had time, of course, to get out of the hedge and start walking the other way, but he didn't have time to conceal his binoculars. Then he fed me some story about how he was a keen birdwatcher, and he pointed at some goldfinches in a bush and called them gold tits, which don't exist, and got the name of the bush wrong,' recounted Lou.

'I would put money on it that he was spying on us, the question is, why?'

None of them could find a satisfactory answer to that. They agreed that they needed to be on their guard. It was a pity because suddenly their holiday didn't seem quite so much fun.

'Let's not bother to do any more metal detecting today,' said Lou. 'I'm not in the mood. How about we go back to the lake and do some swimming? If we go to the spot overhung by those reeds and bulrushes, that man shouldn't be able to see us even if he does come spying.

'Jack, David – the three of us will take it in turns, however, to peek through the trees surrounding the lake, to see if there is anyone prowling around. Is that ok?'

They both nodded. Lou always knew what to do for the best. They changed into their swimming things and put jeans and T-shirts on top. With their towels stuffed into rucksacks they headed off. Lou took the metal detector with her, making sure that Mr Fitzgerald would see her, should he be watching from within his tent flaps.

He had, she noticed, positioned his tent so that it looked directly towards their campsite. Well let him get curious and follow, the more they learnt about what he was up to, the better.

CHAPTER EIGHT

Drama in the hidden lake

THEIR spirits lifted the moment they set eyes on the lake, hidden from view behind trees and shrubs, like their campsite. It glittered like a great oval-shaped diamond as the sun's rays broke across its surface. The children went to the eastern shore where the bank dropped sharply out of sight behind great bulrushes and reeds.

'Aren't bulrushes strange with those big brown, furry tubes with a spike sticking out,' said Emily, who had sat in the shallow part. 'They're like big long kebabs on sticks aren't they?'

'I suppose,' said Lou. 'I've never thought of them like that before. Anyway, the "kebab" bit is made up of loads of tiny flowers and seeds – try breaking one and millions of bits of white fluff will float up in clouds – actually don't, we'll end up being covered in it.

'Right, let's go swimming she added, 'I could do with some exercise. Race you to the other bank!'

Jack and David took her up on the challenge but were beaten easily. Lou had always been athletic – and always came top of her class at school for sports like swimming and running.

'Come on Emily!' shouted Lou, grinning. 'Stop sitting there daydreaming and do some proper swimming.'

Emily wouldn't budge so Lou swam across and began to splash her with water.

'Ugh, get off you bully,' cried Emily, laughing as she staggered to her feet and waded into the deeper water.

'Get swimming,' retorted Lou, giving her a friendly shove.

Emily wasn't quite ready for that and toppled over into

the reeds catching her finger on one of them. Their edges were surprisingly sharp.

'Ouch!' she said, 'that hurt. Be careful!'

'Oh Emily, you've cut your finger,' exclaimed Lou.

Emily looked at the second finger of her right hand and cried out in dismay. It wasn't the pain from the cut which distressed her.

'My ring, oh my lovely golden ring with little diamonds that my parents gave me for my 10th birthday. It's missing! It must have been yanked off when that reed caught my finger.'

Huge tears welled in Emily's eyes. This was not turning out to be a great day. Lou looked distressed. Not only had she caused that accident, Emily had now lost a cherished and valuable gold ring. Lou looked stunned and crestfallen.

Emily crouched and began desperately to scrabble in the silt floor of the lake bottom with the other hand.

'Now listen Emily,' said Lou. 'That's no use, all you'll do is make it harder to find. You come out and get your hand bandaged. I've got a first aid kit in my rucksack. I've also got some goggles. I will put them on and dive to the bed of the lake and keep searching until I find that ring. I am so sorry, it's all my stupid fault.'

Emily stepped gingerly from the water and Jack went and got a towel which he threw over her shoulders. Noting carefully where exactly Emily had been standing, Lou led her up onto the bank. After bandaging her finger, she pulled on her goggles.

'Jack and David, you look after Emily. I am going to dive down to see if I can find that ring,' she said.

'Would it help to have the trowel?' said Jack, anxious to be useful.

'Yes, that's a good idea,' she replied. 'Look, why don't you lot get back to the camp and I'll join you in a bit.'

Jack and David led Emily away. They got themselves

dry in the trees and put some clothes on.

'It's ok Lou,' shouted Emily as Lou slipped back into the lake. 'It was an accident, don't worry.'

That was kind of Emily but in her heart she was very sad to lose that precious ring. It meant more to her than almost anything. Lou knew that and had no intention of coming out of the water until she had found it, even if it took her hours.

She waved goodbye to the others then, with a look of determination on her face, took a deep breath and swam to the lake bottom. It was covered in silt, like a fine sand. That was bad news – any small object such as a ring would easily disappear from sight. She had to hope she might see a faint glimmer from it.

Lou could only spend 30 or 40 seconds at a time before she had to come up for air. Also, it was impossible to be sure that she wasn't searching the same area twice. Down she went, a second time, a third time, a fourth time. Each time she came up, gasping for air, no further forward. Again and again she dived to the lake bottom.

Unhelpfully, the sun chose that moment to disappear behind a cloud. Without it she wouldn't have a hope of seeing a glint of gold or a sparkle of diamond.

She was about to get out onto the bank for a break when, to her horror, she glimpsed sight of Mr Fitzgerald in between the trees. She crouched amid the thick reeds and bulrushes. From what she could see, the annoying man appeared to be making his way down from the trees to the lakeside itself.

Sure enough, he began to stroll around it. This was worrying. When he got the other side, he would be able to see her. She pulled herself as deeply as she could into the bank, behind some thick, tall bulrushes which would hopefully block his view. She tried to sink her bottom into the silt so that as little of her protruded above the water as possible.

The sun chose that moment to come out from behind the cloud. Lou held her breath. If he looked hard, he would see bits of her through the reeds. He seemed not to notice. Whether he had come for an innocent stroll around the lake or to find out what they were up to she couldn't say, but he continued his walk, holding his hands behind his back, his tweed cap pulled firmly over his large ears and, then by all accounts, disappeared.

Lou stayed exactly where she was. She wanted to give him plenty of time to clear off. The sun beat down hard now on the water and Lou gazed gloomily across it, dreading having to return and tell Emily she had failed to find her ring. She sat there, almost in a trance under the sun's hot rays.

Every now and then, the tiniest glimmer caught her eye. At first, she assumed it was merely the sun's reflection on the water's surface but it wasn't strong enough for that. The glimmer appeared to come from beyond the big toe of her left foot. Yes, she was sure of it. Something was catching the light down there!

If it was the ring, it was in much shallower water than she'd been looking in. Could it have slipped off before Emily waded deeper? That was good news. But if she dived for it, she risked disturbing the lake floor and causing clouds of silt to rise up. She could easily lose it.

Lou had an idea. She could just about extend her foot above the spot. She clamped her toes hard on the glimmer. Then she inched her body forward. She was almost out of her depth now and struggling to keep her head above water.

She could feel something smooth and hard in between her toes! This was promising.

I'll bring my foot slowly up, keeping my toes clamped tight, thought Lou at first. That risked dropping whatever it was. She had to push her hand underneath her foot and take the chance that it would disturb the sediment. There was nothing else for it. She thrust herself forwards and grabbed at the hard object underneath. The movement caused a swirl of silt to rise upwards, clouding the water.

To her immense disappointment, she found herself clutching the neck of an old glass bottle of some kind. It was sealed and entirely opaque so she had no clue what, if anything, was inside it. Nor did she care – the ring still eluded her. What a pity!

She was about to get up when she realised that she still had her toes clamped tight. It may have been her imagination, but she felt sure she could still feel something else hard between her toes. She tightened them and whatever it was dug into the sole of her foot. Not wishing to risk lunging for it now that she had the bottle in one hand, she dragged herself backwards towards the bank, keeping her foot clenched. She hauled her bottom out onto the clay bank and then gingerly reached her free hand down to the object gripped between her toes. It was probably a stone, she told herself.

It wasn't. It was a rather heavy band of smooth metal with knobbly bits around the middle. Lou held it in her palm, not daring to look at it at first, willing it to be the ring, Emily's precious ring.

The sun, which had temporarily disappeared behind a cloud, sailed out again and Lou opened her hand.

'Yes!' she exclaimed. It *was* Emily's ring, more bright and beautiful than ever since it was soaking wet. It glistened and dazzled beautifully in the sun. She looked in delight at it, then at the strange bottle she held in her other hand. It was curious, she would take that back to show the others, too.

What a stroke of luck! If it hadn't been for Mr Fitzgerald creeping about, she would never have stayed still long enough to see the ring glimmering in the sun's rays. How strange that it had not sunk into the sediment, out of sight. It must have come to land on the old bottle when it slipped from Emily's finger.

Lou glanced about her as she pulled herself from the water and retrieved her things from under a bush. No-one was in sight. She pushed the ring deep into her purse and zipped it carefully in her rucksack. She could not bear to lose it a second time! As for the strange bottle, she shoved that into a side pocket and thought no more about it.

She towelled herself quickly and got dressed, then strolled cheerfully back across the ploughed field and into their own. She felt so pleased, she couldn't even feel any annoyance at seeing Mr Fitzgerald's bright red tent a few dozen yards away from their campsite.

She couldn't wait to see Emily's face when she told her the good news!

CHAPTER NINE

Astonishing discovery

'OH Lou, you've been gone ages, we've been getting worried,' said Emily, when Lou slipped through the poplar trees and joined them. 'I'll boil the kettle for you and make you a nice hot brew. You're shivering, poor thing.'

Emily was right. Lou *was* shivering. She had spent too long in chilly water in what had nearly proved to be a long and fruitless search.

'Thank you so much for looking for the ring, you've done your best and please don't feel bad about it. It's one of those things, that's all. Come and sit down. I'll get you a thick jumper from the tent.'

Lou sat on a tree stump as Emily brought her a woolly jumper which she gratefully pulled on. With the shade from the trees, the day was getting cooler.

'Oh I'm looking forward to that cup of tea,' she said. 'It was hard work searching for that ring.'

'No problem, cuppa coming right up,' said Emily, putting the kettle on the stove and doing her best to sound cheerful.

'Aren't you going to ask me whether I found it or not?' said Lou, her green eyes sparkling mischievously.

'You didn't? Oh Lou you couldn't possibly have?' exclaimed Emily, staring at her in amazement. 'You were gone so long, we had given up any hope.'

'I've got it,' said Lou. 'I had given up hope too, I did everything I could to find it, and then in the end it was a sheer fluke.'

Lou pulled her purse from the rucksack and carefully extracted the ring. Emily burst into tears when she saw it in the palm of Lou's hand.

'Oh Lou, what can I say, you're wonderful. I don't know how to thank you. You absolute star.'

'I'm not,' retorted Lou. 'I'm the clot who lost it in the first place. How's your poor finger?'

'It's a fine cut, it will be gone overnight,' said Emily giving Lou a big hug and nearly spilling her tea. 'Oh what a wonderful end to a rather strange day.'

'That reminds me,' said Lou, 'talking of strange. I also found a funny old bottle in exactly the same spot as your ring. In fact, I think it was the reason I managed to. The ring must have fallen on top of it and still been visible. The bottle was right underneath.'

She held it up for the others to see.

'What do you suppose it is?' she said. 'It doesn't look modern at all.'

They looked at the glass object, puzzled. It was entirely opaque, yet it might originally have been made of clear glass and become scratched to the point where its surface was frosted over. Its neck was sealed. There was no way of opening it. Yet when they shook it, there was clearly something inside, something which rattled slightly and looked as if it might be yellowish in colour.

'I found the ring with the bottle underneath while hiding deep in the reeds and bulrushes because guess who I saw come spooking around the water's edge? None other than our fellow camper Mr Fitzgerald!' said Lou.

'It's funny you should say that,' said Jack, taking the strange bottle from her and examining it as he spoke. 'You're right, there's no way of opening it, what a pity. Anyway, we have some news you'll be interested in.'

'Go on,' said Lou.

'Well, as we came out from the trees around the lake and began walking back across the ploughed field to our campsite, who do you think we should see in the middle of the field?'

'The spooky Mr Fitzgerald, by any chance?' asked Lou.

'That's right and what do you think he was up to?' replied Jack.

'I have no idea,' said Lou, impatiently. 'Admiring the red tits perhaps, or the purple finches or the farmyard geese which he thought were swans? You tell me.'

'No,' said Jack, pausing for dramatic effect. 'He was walking up and down with headphones on and swishing away with his very own metal detector. What do you think of that!'

'You're joking!' said Lou, astonished. 'So he's got his own metal detector here too and had the cheek to use it, right in the spot where we've been looking? Do the farmer and his wife know about this I wonder? I'll bet they don't. What on earth is he playing at?'

She looked from Jack to David to the others. Their faces were blank. They had no idea either.

Before any of them had a chance to speak, a harsh, sneering voice rang out somewhere amid the trees.

'I'm sure my parents have no problem with Mr Fitzgerald having a go with his metal detector – after all, they've let you.'

The others swung round to find Becky suddenly appearing out of nowhere. They looked at her furiously. How long had she been eavesdropping on their conversation?

'What do you want?' snapped Lou.

'I've come to check that you're all happy campers,' said Becky, with a maddening grin on her face. 'You must be relieved that Mr Fitzgerald has turned up to camp as well, so you've got a guardian to watch over you and make sure you're safe.

'I've asked him to keep a look out for you and help you out. Perhaps he could give you some tips on how to go metal detecting, since you don't seem to be getting very far!'

The others glared at Becky. How dare she march into their campsite like this and start throwing her weight around in this way?

'You're a fool,' said Lou, quietly. 'You know nothing about that Mr Fitzgerald and your whole purpose for letting him camp here was to annoy us, for no good reason. If by any chance he does now come upon the Anglo-Saxon treasure we have been seeking, then my guess is he will make off with the lot of it. There'll be no sharing it 50-50 with your parents. He'll be gone with it faster than you can blink. You won't be wearing that silly smirk then, will you?'

'Don't you call me a fool,' snapped back Becky, furiously. That thought hadn't occurred to her but she wasn't going to let them know that.

'Why not,' chipped in Jack, 'because that's exactly what you are.'

The others nodded.

Becky tossed back her luxuriant mane of wavy chestnut hair, of which she was very proud, and pursed her lips, painted with a particularly bright lipstick.

'I am the daughter of the owner of the land on which you are camping. I would strongly advise you not to insult me or you are likely to find yourself evicted,' she said in a self-important and snooty tone.

'It is you who is likely to be evicted from this land if your parents can't make it pay,' said Lou in a quiet, almost hypnotic monotone. 'The money we have paid to camp here will help them and there is a chance – however small – that our metal detecting might turn up something valuable.'

'You don't know what you're talking about and it is none of your business anyway,' said Becky, her top lip quivering somewhat.

Lou could be harsh and unforgiving at times, but Becky needed to be told some home truths.

'You are a silly, childish girl who behaves like a 10-year-old,' said Lou. 'I cannot believe you're 14.'

That was a direct hit and Becky turned a deep red with rage. She prided herself on looking as grown-up as possible, wearing make-up and copying the sulky, rebellious attitude of some of the bigger girls in her school.

'How dare you!' screeched Becky. 'Look at the fashionable clothes I wear. Take a look at my hair and jewellery. I could pass for 16 easily. Then look at you lot in your shabby jeans and T-shirts. You're just a bunch of kids. As for you two,' she added, looking disdainfully at Lou and Emily, 'I don't suppose you even know what lipstick is.'

'Do you think wearing that dreadful red lipstick makes you a grown up?' said Lou contemptuously. 'I wouldn't touch it if you paid me. Now why don't you run along back to mummy and daddy before you get any mud on those nice suede boots.'

'You do not – I repeat you do *not* tell me what to do. I am two years older than you and you are camping on my land. Any more rudeness and I shall ask my parents to remove you.'

'You are pathetic and we have no more to say to you. Now clear off, you're spoiling our evening,' replied Lou with infuriating calm.

'Apologise for calling me pathetic,' demanded Becky.

'Certainly not, clear off,' came Lou's brusque retort.

'Apologise now!' yelled Becky.

Lou ignored her completely. So did the others. Becky stood there, red-faced and glowering, shaking with rage but not knowing what to do or say. How maddening it was that she was being humiliated by some girl two years younger than her.

'I'm waiting,' was all Becky could think to say.

Lou had had enough. She got up and moved towards Becky, intending to get her by the arm and frog-march her out of their campsite. At that moment, Becky grabbed the strange glass bottle from the lake which Lou had put down on a tree stump. Becky had no idea what it was, only that it was hard enough to hurt. She threw it with all her might at Lou.

Lou ducked just in time and it connected at speed with the trunk of a tree, breaking into several pieces. The others looked at Becky in horror. What a terrible, violent thing to do!

Becky turned tail and fled, realising the anger she had caused. She had horrified herself at acting that way. She could have really hurt Lou.

'Lou are you ok,' shouted Jack, bounding over to her.

'I'm fine, I ducked didn't I?' said Lou. But she wasn't fine, she was shaking. She knew she could have been wounded by Becky and for a moment felt rather scared and vulnerable, and Lou didn't often feel like that.

'Be careful of stepping on any shards of broken glass, Jack,' said Lou, trying to recover her composure.

'Hang on a minute, whatever's that,' said David, pointing.

At the foot of the poplar tree which had taken the hit, amid pieces of thick whitish glass was what looked like a tightly-rolled up napkin. It must have fallen from the old bottle when it smashed.

'You pick it up David, I want to sit quiet for a bit,' said Lou, unsteadily.

He did so and stared at it curiously. On closer inspection, the 'napkin' was thick, yellowed parchment. As gently as he could, he unravelled it.

What looked like a brooch slid out! It was fashioned from gold with a bright red precious stone in the middle, circular discs of coloured glass around its edge and intricate patterns interwoven on its surface. The children gasped in astonishment. They had never seen anything like it before, so beautiful and ancient.

'Look – there is writing on that parchment,' said Lou. 'A fine, elegant script but it doesn't look quite like English. Is it Latin perhaps?'

The four of them did not speak for several seconds. They simply gazed in wonder at the parchment and the brooch, as if they could not quite believe what was in front of them.

Then Lou looked across at David. 'Do you think this might possibly be Anglo Saxon, and something to do with the missing hoard?'

Emily clutched Jack's shoulder in excitement. The others looked at David. If anyone would know, then surely he might. He was the one who had spent so many hours, his head buried in books, absorbing all that was known about the great find of Anglo-Saxon treasure in farmland a couple of miles away from where they were camping. And it was David who had uncovered the references to a missing hoard in an old Victorian book on antiquities, gathering dust in the loft.

'I don't know for sure,' he said, slowly and rather monotonously, as if in a trance. 'I can only guess.'

'Then guess,' prompted Lou.

'My feeling is that it may be from that period. I thought the bottle this was sealed in looked to be ancient glass – of course now that vandal Becky has smashed it, we may never know. This parchment is clearly dried animal skin of the type used in the days before they had paper. The writing upon it, I would think, looks written in an early version of our alphabet – which the Anglo Saxons began to use from the seventh century onwards.

'The Staffordshire Hoard is thought to date from around that time.'

'Can you read any of it?' asked Emily.

'No,' replied David. 'It's not just the handwriting and the unusual letters, it isn't the sort of English we write today. It looks like it might be Old English – which is what the Anglo Saxons would have used.

'As for this brooch – it also looks centuries old. The patterning, and the use of that red precious stone – garnet I think it's called – is a feature of Anglo-Saxon jewellery. Also, remember that the Staffordshire Hoard contained only male, military items. This brooch would probably have been worn by a woman. So possibly, this parchment and brooch are relics from that missing second hoard thought to contain female and domestic items.'

The others listened, most impressed. David could be remarkably brainy when he wanted to be. True, they often pulled his leg about learning Welsh and constantly having his head in books, but he was fast becoming very knowledgeable.

'Good,' said Lou. 'This is an astonishing discovery. We now need to decide what to do tomorrow. I think finding this parchment rather changes things a bit. For all we know it might hold the key to the whereabouts of the missing hoard. I certainly think it is worth checking out. After all, we haven't exactly had much luck metal detecting across the ploughed field so far, have we?'

'Also,' pointed out Jack, 'do you remember what we were telling you, Lou, before we were so rudely interrupted by Becky? The creepy Mr Fitzgerald has got his own metal detector and is searching that very field.'

'Yes of course,' said Lou. 'That had slipped my mind. I find that fishy you know. It seems a strange coincidence that he should wish to come here and do that within a day of us arriving. It's almost as if he knew of our mission.

'One thing's for sure, we can't easily stop him so I suggest we don't try. Let's go to Lichfield tomorrow to the library or somewhere and see if we can find someone able to help us translate this parchment. In a place steeped in history like Lichfield, I'll bet there'll be someone who will understand it.'

'So we leave Fitzgerald to treasure hunt to his heart's

content?' asked Jack, frowning a little.

'Oh hang on, I've got an idea,' said Emily excitedly, blushing slightly. 'Well, you know since we've been here we've collected rather a lot of tin cans from our campfire meals? I've been putting them to one side in a box to put in the farm's recycling bin.

'How about we sneak back to the ploughed field tonight when it's dark and bury them all over the place? Then when Mr Fitzgerald starts metal detecting tomorrow he'll spend half the day digging useless metal back up again.'

'Brilliant!' exclaimed Lou. 'That's a wonderful idea, Emily. Jack, how about you and me go later on – it'll be dark by about 10 now it's so nearly September. With any luck there'll be some moonlight to see by.'

The thought of creepy Mr Fitzgerald spending hours digging up tin cans kept the children chortling merrily through their campfire supper. As shadows lengthened and the sun disappeared for the day, Lou and Jack quietly sneaked out through the trees armed with a huge bag of cans and a spade each.

Mr Fitzgerald had been combing the field as they had, north to south, so they guessed approximately where he had got to and then started burying the cans at regular intervals – spacing some near each other to make it particularly hard for him to know exactly where to dig.

'Isn't it spooky out here, in the middle of a big, empty field under moonlight,' said Jack to Lou. 'Your face looks ghostly white.'

'Oh you're saying I look like a ghost?' retorted Lou, grinning. 'Maybe I should wear lots of make-up and lipstick like Becky.'

Jack shuddered. 'Please don't,' he said. 'We like you the way you are.'

'Thanks Jack,' said Lou. 'We're a good team aren't we – and all thanks to our chance meeting at Abersoch.'

‘Lou,’ said Jack, resting on his spade for a minute, ‘we will meet up again at Abersoch won’t we – you’ll go there again next year for summer holidays? It’s just,’ he hesitated for a minute. ‘When you’re not around I miss you, we all do.’

‘I miss you lot too,’ said Lou, softly. ‘I live in the middle of nowhere remember. We can meet up at Easter and in autumn and plenty of other times, as well as summer. You’ll never get rid of me now!’

She gave his arm a squeeze. ‘Anyway, that’s the last tin can, let’s get back to the others and get to bed,’ she said. ‘Tomorrow should prove an interesting day.’

CHAPTER TEN

Successful day out

'LICHFIELD isn't really big enough to be a city is it?' said Emily, as they cycled into the city centre, her long, blonde hair flowing out behind her.

'It isn't just about how big a place is,' said Lou. 'Anyway, I hate big cities, this is about the right sort of size if you ask me.'

Jack and David also looked around them approvingly. All four of them had grown up in villages, although Lou's home in Shropshire was far more remote than theirs. None of them were used to big built-up places with endless rows of houses and factories.

Occasionally Lou would travel to Shrewsbury, the county town of Shropshire, and the others would go shopping to Chester. But sprawling urban areas were unfamiliar to them and they were rather relieved that the 'city' of Lichfield was not like that.

It was an attractive, well-kept place, with many interesting and charming buildings. Some were half-timbered and looked as though they dated back hundreds of years – which they probably did.

Lou had the parchment safely zipped into the pocket of her rucksack. They were eager to find out what the writing said and whether it might give any clue to the missing Anglo-Saxon treasure.

The big challenge of course, would be to find someone who could understand Old English of the sort used more than a thousand years ago. They went to the library first – it was a large, impressive building and seemed the sort of place where scholars of long-forgotten languages would be found.

The librarian, a rather elderly, silver-haired woman was kind and anxious to be helpful. She couldn't think of anyone in the building at that moment able to translate seventh-century Old English, however.

'I wonder,' she said, pursing up her lips as she thought hard, 'whether someone at the Samuel Johnson Birthplace Museum might be able to help. I don't know if you're aware, but Dr Samuel Johnson is one of Lichfield's most famous literary sons. He didn't just compile England's first major dictionary, but wrote many other things of great note.'

'Thank you, we'll try there,' said Lou, anxious to avoid a long speech on the literary merits of Dr Johnson.

The museum staff couldn't help either. They suggested going to the cathedral which, they pointed out, actually dated from around the same time as the Staffordshire Hoard.

The children cycled off along the winding, narrow streets of Lichfield's historic centre towards the cathedral. They looked up in wonder when they saw it, a towering, mediaeval structure set in its own grounds with a court-yard and centuries-old buildings facing it, several half-timbered with striking, low hanging roofs and quaint lampposts dotted around in bright, polished black.

'It's like stepping back in time,' said David, approvingly. 'It's so unspoilt and untouched by modernity. Imagine what this scene would look like covered in snow, with a robin perched in a bush. It would look like a Christmas card.' The others nodded and paused to imagine such a pleasant scene.

'It's also an important place of course in the Church of England,' added David, knowledgeably, although he didn't know why.

'The question is, will anyone inside be able to help us translate this document?' said Lou, 'it certainly looks like our best hope.'

The children tiptoed silently inside the cathedral. They were more used to small, rural churches and the sheer size of it took their breath away. They spent a few minutes walking up the nave and gazing up at its splendour.

'Oh look,' whispered Emily. 'Do you think that man might be able to help us? He's wearing a black robe with a white collar. He must be a priest of some kind.'

They went over to speak to him. He was a senior priest, the Very Reverend Adrian Farthing – the Cathedral Dean. He was in overall charge of the cathedral. He wasn't stuffy or unfriendly. He seemed delighted to come across a group of children taking such an interest in the place. They told him of their quest and, rather to Lou's surprise, he said that he might be able to help.

'You see, a long time ago, when I was training for the clergy and undertaking a degree in theology, I studied ancient and classical languages, including Old English, Latin and Greek,' explained the Dean. 'So I might be of some use to you – provided that I can follow the handwriting on the parchment.

'Come with me into my little office here and show me, it sounds fascinating. I will be most interested to see it and that brooch of which you speak.'

The children took to the Dean at once, with his friendly, jolly face and cheerful smile. He made them feel relaxed, understanding that they were a bit scared of being in such a big and important cathedral. It's funny how with some people you know instantly whether they are good eggs or bad eggs.

'We are lucky enough to have one or two Anglo-Saxon treasures ourselves here, and we were also allowed to host the exhibition of items from the Staffordshire Hoard here in 2011,' he said.

The Very Reverend Mr Farthing whistled in astonishment when Lou carefully took out the two artefacts from the smashed bottle and placed them on the table.

‘That brooch is almost certainly Anglo Saxon,’ he said, firmly, ‘It is a remarkably well preserved specimen. Fancy it being stuck in that bottle for so many countless years. Tell me, how did it get smashed, exactly?’

‘It’s a long story,’ sighed Lou. She was slightly reluctant to divulge what happened but the Dean was clearly a trustworthy, decent sort so she told him what happened.

‘Now we are left with this strange parchment, wondering whether it might hold the key to finding a second Staffordshire Hoard,’ she said.

‘Right, let’s take a good look,’ said the Dean. ‘Goodness gracious, this writing is difficult to follow in places, although it is beautifully done. I wish I could write so well.

‘I tell you what, children, this may take me some time but it is a remarkable find and I would love to decipher what I can of it for you. May I possibly take a photocopy of it and have a jolly good go at working it out while you get yourselves some lunch perhaps? It is nearly that time of day after all. Then come back to me this afternoon and I’ll tell you what I’ve found out.’

That sounded an excellent idea to the others who were getting peckish by now. Emily was convinced her tummy would start rumbling in a minute and in a huge, echoey place like a cathedral, everybody would be sure to hear.

They left the clergyman to his task and walked from the cathedral in the direction of a small café he had recommended in the Close nearby. They got themselves a table and ordered a light snack and a cup of coffee each.

‘This is the perfect place for a coffee,’ said Emily. ‘At the campsite, tea is a much better drink but here, it’s got to be coffee hasn’t it?’

The others agreed. It was good too – freshly brewed which tasted as rich as it smelt.

‘Fingers crossed the vicar chap can help us,’ said Jack. ‘I know we never came here with much hope of finding the treasure but now that we are on the trail with Mr Fitzgerald seemingly searching for the same thing I feel determined that we do whatever we can. Above all, I'd hate him to find it before us.'

'The question is,' said Lou, taking a slurp of her coffee, 'is he actually searching for the same thing and if so, what prompted his sudden interest? How come this man appeared out of nowhere, camping right on top of us at a farm which does not usually take campers, claiming to be a birdwatcher when he doesn't have a clue about birds? Why does he watch our every move and why is he scouring the field that we are interested in? It seems too much of a coincidence to me. It doesn't add up.'

'Perhaps,' said David, 'he is quite an authority himself on antiquities and the Staffordshire Hoard and has himself come across information which suggests there might be a missing second hoard in that field.'

'Hmm,' said Lou, deep in thought. 'How odd though, that this brings him here a day after us. It is almost as if he followed us here, and has known our intentions all along.'

That made Emily shiver. 'Oh don't say that Lou, it makes me feel scared.'

'There's no need to be scared, Emily,' reassured Lou. 'The man isn't dangerous like those smugglers in North Wales – he won't do us any harm. The danger lies in the fact that he seems to know what we are after and is determined to get to it first. It may be that the theory about the missing hoard is not such a long-lost secret as we thought and that he and possibly others try every now and again to find it.'

'The farmer and his wife made no mention of anyone else seeking it out – not on their land anyway,' pointed out David. 'As you say, it wouldn't explain why he arrived here so soon after we did.'

'We need to be extremely alert and on our guard with

him,' said Lou, firmly. 'He may, for instance, have trailed us to Lichfield today without us knowing – and we left the farmyard this morning without so much as a glance over our shoulders. We ought to be constantly checking all around us and looking out for him. It's worth being careful.'

They gazed out of the big café windows towards the towering cathedral. For a moment they felt like Mr Fitzgerald might suddenly emerge from behind a drain pipe or a gargoyle or something. There wasn't any sign of him.

Suddenly Jack chuckled and grinned at Lou. 'I think I know where Mr Fitzgerald is likely to be today,' he said.

Lou hooted with laughter too. 'Yes of course,' she said, 'with any luck he'll be scurrying up and down that ploughed field like a mad thing, desperately trying to find the treasure before we get back only to dig up one tin can after another after another. It's baking hot too, he'll be sweating buckets in that thick tweed. He'll be absolutely furious!'

'Even so, he may find the treasure in our absence,' cautioned Emily.

'He may and he may not. We will have well and truly slowed him to a crawl,' said Lou. 'Do you know the funny thing? I'm not too sure the hoard is in that field any more. I have a feeling that when we've deciphered the writing on that parchment it might point us in a totally different direction.'

They strolled around the city centre for a while, to give the kindly priest plenty of time to do what he could to translate the document. By 3pm they couldn't wait any longer and walked eagerly back into the cathedral. The Dean was in his office and beckoned them to come in.

'Take a seat,' he said, beaming at them, 'and we will go through this writing line by line. I have typed out what I think each word says in the original Old English and I've done you a copy so you can show it to a rather better scholar than me.

'Here is my interpretation of what it says in modern English. I've got you a copy of that too, that you can take away with you.'

The children pored over both documents. The typed-up Old English was still incomprehensible to them – it was effectively a different language – but the Dean's translation was startlingly clear:

Know ye, fellow men of Mercia who dig this spot. This is no longer safe for the land is marsh and the water (= pool or lake) grows ever bigger. Seek the underground caves due east. It is not far. Down the tunnel, keep straight then left and left again into the cave. Behind the great stalactite high up, is a rock shelf. Up there will ye find what ye seek. The rest remains buried in the same spot, south of the Roman Road.

'What do you make of that?' said the Dean looking steadily at each one of them. 'Do you know of these caves?'

'No,' said Lou. 'We have not come across them.'

'I think I might know,' said Emily, suddenly. 'I was chatting to Mrs Owen yesterday when I called round for some milk and eggs. We got talking about the farm and she was telling me some of its history and its interesting features.'

'Go on,' said Lou, impatiently.

'Well she told me about the sandstone rocks around their fields to the east. The sandstone towers up in a great ridge, forming a natural border to their land. She said that there were underground passages which had been cut through the soft sandstone. She didn't say anything about any caves but perhaps she doesn't know about them.'

'How interesting,' said the Dean. 'Well if you ask me, that may well be the location that this parchment refers to. What I think has happened, if you'll permit me to put forward my theory, is that the Anglo-Saxon tribe which buried the treasure in the field to the east of the lake on what is now Mr and Mrs Owen's farm, became troubled at the encroachment of water – possibly from the lake itself – or perhaps they thought the land was prone to flood.

'So they removed the hoard to a safe location – and what better place to choose than natural underground hollows? They reburied this bottle in the same spot to let other tribe members know. Their fears were thence borne out – the lake expanded over that area.'

'Which is why Lou found the bottle in the lake itself – and on the eastern side, in shallow water, by accident while looking for my ring,' said Emily, her cornflower-blue eyes shining with excitement.

'I am sure that if your ring hadn't been sitting on top of that jutting out bottle, I wouldn't have found it – or the bottle,' pointed out Lou. 'Perhaps that bottle and its contents is a good omen. The question is, will the Anglo-Saxon treasure still be in its new resting place inside the underground cave, or will it be long gone?'

'Aah, who knows?' replied the Dean. 'Possibly, in the many hundreds of years which have passed, others will have been down and plundered the site but it is doubtless not a place which is visited frequently.'

'Anyway,' said Lou, 'if that bottle was buried as a guide for other members of the same tribe then it was clearly never discovered by them. No-one, it would appear, has ever had any reason to believe that treasure has been stored on a stone shelf inside an underground cave.'

'It sounds to me like your next move is to go down those tunnels and find out – if it's safe to do so, of course,' said the Dean. 'You mustn't take any risks.'

'Thank you so much for your help with this,' said Lou, her striking green eyes looking gratefully at him from under her dark fringe. 'You've been amazing.'

'It's wonderful to be involved,' said the Dean, beaming. 'Do please tell me how you got on, I would love to know – particularly as our cathedral has such links with the Anglo-Saxon era and we have had items from the Staffordshire Hoard on display here for the public to look at.'

'We promise you faithfully that if we find anything, we'll make sure that you can display items from the second Staffordshire Hoard, isn't that right David?' said Lou. 'It was David's brains and detective work which got us on the trail in the first place.'

David agreed. He was looking excited, as were the others, and it was a happy bunch of children who cycled the three-mile journey back to Wall.

'I think this is great news,' enthused Lou as they whizzed along Claypit Lane past the field of brilliant yellow flowers. 'There has got to be a chance that the treasure is still there and better still, Mr Fitzgerald won't know a thing about it. He can carry on searching that field to his heart's content unaware that he is wasting his time.'

The others chuckled at that, although Jack pointed out that they shouldn't get their hopes up too much. There was probably a better than even chance that someone had discovered its hiding place sometime in the last 1,200 years.

'It's better than no chance at all,' retorted Lou. 'There are times when we have to trust to luck and hope that it holds, and often it does.'

'I think you make your own good luck, Lou, because you're so confident and capable,' said Emily. 'I would never have thought to try and get that old parchment translated. I'm still hoping I'll be like you one day.'

Lou laughed. 'I've told you before Emily, don't hope any such thing,' she said, putting her hand out to indicate a right to turn into the farmyard. I'm hard-faced in some ways, a bit like that Becky, and you're a sweetie. I don't want you to change. In fact, I don't want any of you to change. You're all great!'

'And you're the greatest of the lot,' said Jack, as he and the others turned into the farmyard after her.

'Well, there's praise,' came a sour-faced voice. It was Becky, swinging on the farm gate.

CHAPTER ELEVEN

Becky gets nasty

'A GREAT nuisance more like – as you all are. Where have you been today, we've missed you,' Becky added, sarcastically. 'I'm surprised you haven't spent all day out treasure hunting.'

'We thought we'd give it a miss and go off to explore Lichfield today,' said Lou.

'Oh that'd be right, walking around the shops together, playing at being grown-up and independent. Did you try on some clothes and then make an excuse for not wanting to buy anything?' asked Becky, with her trademark curled lip.

'What we did was none of your business,' stated Jack, firmly and coldly.

Lou shot him an admiring glance. Jack was becoming more grown up, and that wasn't play acting. He had put Becky in her place, where she deserved to be and Jack wouldn't usually be confident enough to do that.

'Oh hark at him!' countered Becky, sauntering over and standing in front of them with her hands on her hips. Glancing at Lou, she said, 'goodness me, hasn't your little helper got tough all of a sudden?'

'Do you want anything Becky, because we're going back to our campsite now. We've had a lovely day out and we don't want it ruined by a spoilt child like you,' said Lou, wearily.

'Do you know what I wish,' said Becky, screwing her nose up and narrowing her eyes at Lou. 'I wish that bottle I threw at you yesterday had connected with your head and left you with a nice cut to your pretty little face.'

'That could have seriously hurt me, do you realise that.

You really are unpleasant, aren't you?' said Lou, shocked. 'Just get out of our way, we're going back to our tents.'

'Don't you tell me to get out of your way when you're on my land, you cheeky moo,' snapped Becky.

Unable to go forwards, since Becky blocked her path, Lou attempted to steer around her. As she did so, Becky put her foot out and jabbed it hard against the hub of Lou's front wheel.

The bike gave way beneath her and toppled over with a crash and a clatter to the muddy farmyard floor.

A couple of passing geese looked up in surprise as Lou yelled in pain. Jack and David dismounted and rushed to help. Lou looked dazed and dishevelled, with mud down her side. Her right cheek was grazed and trickled with blood and she'd been badly bruised.

'Look what you've done! You ought to be ashamed of yourself,' said Emily, glaring at Becky.

'It was only a push,' said Becky, shrugging. 'It's not my fault she's so clumsy. Right, I better get on. Oh by the way, Mr Fitzgerald has been making good progress metal-detecting in the ploughed field. I reckon he's found a good few ancient artefacts today.'

The others stared at her with scorn bordering on contempt. She had followed up her horrible behaviour with what was almost certainly a straight lie.

For a moment, Lou appeared disorientated; her self-assurance lost in the face of this unruly, temperamental older girl who was clearly prepared to resort to violence when it suited her.

She glanced at Becky and caught her eye. For a fleeting moment she thought she saw a look of shame and regret cross her face. Lou was no longer the headstrong girl for whom Becky felt a mixture of envy and jealousy, but a bedraggled mess.

The four of them walked past Becky without another word, pushing their bikes alongside them. All they wanted was to get back to their campsite as quickly as they could.

Just at that moment, however, Mrs Owen came strolling across the farmyard. She had been to the pigsty feeding the big fat sow and her many piglets.

'Well good afternoon to you all!' she said. 'Have you had a nice day?'

Lou felt embarrassed and humiliated being seen in such a state. They smiled weakly at Mrs Owen.

'Oh my dear, whatever's happened?' said Mrs Owen, looking in horror at Lou.

'It was my fault,' said Lou, before the others had a chance to say anything. I turned into the farmyard too fast and my bike slipped from under me on a muddy patch and I went flying. I'll be ok, I'll jump in the lake and clean myself up.'

'Well why don't you come in the farmhouse and have a hot bath or a shower or something?' said Mrs Owen, kindly. 'You could borrow a couple of Becky's things to wear and a dressing gown or something.'

Lou inwardly shuddered at the prospect of bathing in the farmhouse with Becky gloating outside the door and having to put on her clothes.

'That's nice of you Mrs Owen, but I'll feel much better just going for a quick dip in the lake and having a nice cup of tea from our camping stove.'

Mrs Owen smiled sympathetically. 'As you wish my love. I'm sorry you've had such a fall. I do hope it won't spoil your stay, we've enjoyed having you all here.'

'We're having a great time, honestly, and you've been good to us,' said Lou, who was grateful for her kindness but itching to get away and clean herself up.

In the background, unnoticed, was Becky. She overheard Lou tell her mother that she'd slipped off the bike herself, thereby sparing her a huge telling off.

Becky was baffled why Lou had been willing to do that. She felt guilty and remorseful for her own behaviour.

A tear rolled down her cheek.

As luck wouldn't have it, Mr Fitzgerald happened to be sunning himself in a chair outside his tent as they walked past. He didn't look in the best of spirits though. In fact, he looked worn out. His face was red and his tweed cap hung dejectedly across his forehead.

They tiptoed past, hoping he wouldn't engage them in conversation. Mercifully he didn't, although he appeared to glare at them. They felt relieved when they reached the gently swaying circle of poplars around their campsite.

'Oh Lou, you poor thing are you ok,' said Emily. 'What a bad end to such an enjoyable day.'

'I'll be fine,' said Lou. 'I tell you what, could you get the kettle on while I nip over to the lake and clean up? I'll take a set of clothes. I'll feel loads better when I've washed this mud off me.'

A few minutes later, Lou returned looking much more presentable but still rather deflated. Her cheek was visibly grazed and sore and there was a cut on her hand.

Emily handed her a tin mug brimming with tea and a ginger nut to eat with it. Lou took them gratefully. The others looked at her. It was distressing to see her so low.

'What I can't understand,' said Lou, cradling her hot mug, 'is that not only has Becky chosen to dislike us all, but she seems to particularly dislike me. It just upsets me that's all.'

The others wanted to say something reassuring but Lou had a point. Becky did seem particularly venomous towards her, perhaps it was because she saw her as their leader.

'Anyway, let's not talk about her, she's not worth it. Let's get our evening meal on and discuss our interesting day in Lichfield. Wasn't it an amazing stroke of luck that the cathedral dean was able to translate that document?' said Lou, sounding cheerful once again.

The others cheered up too. Lou was right – blow Becky, there was no point wasting time on her. She was best forgotten about.

Emily was determined to do them a good supper that night. She had some tins of curry, and a pack of rice which she would boil up on the stove, and refreshing, traditional ginger beer to accompany it. The woman in the village shop had chuckled when they bought it, saying they were 'just like the Famous Five'. To Emily, it was rather beginning to feel that way. This camping holiday was at times becoming almost as nerve-wracking as their brush with smugglers at Abersoch and Whistling Sands.

Her culinary efforts were greeted with a round of applause from the others who looked in delight at the fragrant-smelling curry piled high on their tin plates.

'Hmm, smells gorgeous,' cried Lou, as she prepared to take her first forkful. 'And washed down with ginger beer, fantastic.'

It smelt good to Becky too. She was hiding behind one of the poplar trees and the aroma wafting up her nostrils made her feel hungry. How she wished she was sitting there in a circle with them, all friends together and a plateful of curry balanced on her legs. In truth, she would have loved to have become their friend during their stay but somehow felt certain they would not have taken to her. That, combined with suspicion and a brooding envy had led her to show them unremitting hostility.

Becky had gone too far and knew it. She simply had to say sorry. It was a case of choosing the right moment. She had found the courage to walk across to their campsite to apologise yet it hardly seemed right to interrupt them as they were about to eat. She would stay out of sight among the trees and shrubs until they'd finished.

'So, everybody,' mumbled Lou with her mouth half full, 'what's the plan for tomorrow then? I take it we'll be going down those tunnels in the sandstone ridge?'

The others nodded. Their mouths were full, too. Now that they had put the row with Becky to one side, they were starting to enjoy themselves again. They knew they would hardly be able to sleep that night for the excitement of it all.

'We must remember,' cautioned Jack, 'that there is a good chance we'll find nothing. Any number of people must have been along those tunnels and into the caves.'

'Maybe,' said David, 'but there probably won't have been too many – especially not in more recent times since the caves belong to this farmland. There's no public access.'

'Ought we to take some string or something, so we can mark our way?' suggested Emily, sensibly. 'It would be terrible to get lost in there.'

'Yes Emily, you're quite right,' said Lou, 'but chalk would be better, there's no risk of it disappearing. I've got a stick with me in my rucksack, I always keep some. We can mark the walls as we go and it will be easily seen with a good torch. You know, there may or may not be much hope of finding any treasure in those caves but one thing's for sure, we are amazingly lucky to even get this far,' said Lou, pausing for a slurp of her ginger beer.

'What were the chances of me coming across that bottle at the bottom of the lake? Then, even when we found it, it was completely sealed and we wouldn't have been willing to smash it. If it hadn't been for that thug Becky hurling it at me we would never have known of its contents.'

'It's probably the one useful thing she's done in her entire, miserable life,' said Jack.

'Now that was mean of you!' exclaimed Lou, in mock horror. 'On the other hand, it was richly deserved. Don't say it to her face mind, she'll probably lob a rock at you or something.'

The others laughed heartily at this. Lou and Jack were

being cruel, but it was richly deserved.

'Let's hope we do find something tomorrow so that her hard-up parents can benefit financially from it,' added Jack. 'They seem decent people, it's difficult to believe they could have produced such a dreadful daughter.'

The others laughed again. It wasn't nice to speak of anyone in that way but it was perfectly justified. Perhaps, however, they would not have been quite so harsh had they realised that a trembling girl with a mop of chestnut-coloured hair was standing a couple of feet away, over-hearing every word.

Becky's top lip wobbled. She was an only child like Lou, but unlike Lou she had not matured into a tough youngster willing to take all that life threw at her. She was vulnerable and easily crushed by any setback. Their cruel comments about her sliced through her like a knife. The courage she had summoned to go and apologise was evaporating rapidly.

She heard them scraping their tin plates clean. Now was the moment to speak to them if she was going to. Yet they were clearly still angry and upset with her, it would be like entering a lion's den.

Becky hesitated and peeped again through the leaves at them all. At that moment Lou got up and stretched, then she clutched her bruised shoulder and rubbed it. Becky ran away. She didn't have it in her to do the right thing and say sorry. She scampered back down the field towards the farmhouse, feeling worse than ever.

I am pathetic, she told herself. They're right what they say about me.

Their conversation about wanting her parents to get the benefit from any treasure found struck her. How could she have been so wrong about them! Perhaps if she had been more welcoming, she could have accompanied them tomorrow to explore the underground tunnels and caves. Becky had never been near them before. Instead, she was an outcast.

That night, the teenager tossed and turned in her bed, unable to sleep. Eventually she did so after making herself promise to return to the campsite first thing in the morning, and give Lou and the others the apology they were owed.

CHAPTER TWELVE

Fright in the campsite

BECKY'S idea of what constituted 'first thing in the morning' wasn't quite the same as that of the others. Although she lay on a soft mattress rather than a thin groundsheet, it could not make up for the discomfort of a guilty conscience.

Having spent half the night wide awake, Becky then slept solidly until nine o'clock – although that wasn't particularly late for her anyway.

When she did finally rouse herself, she got up promptly, recalling her pledge. But Becky being Becky simply had to have a shower, wash her long, lustrous hair, blow dry it and apply some make-up and lipstick before she went anywhere.

It would also give her more confidence to go and speak to them. She little realised that dolling herself up would serve only to make a poor impression on sensible, down-to-earth children like Lou and the others.

So it was not until 10 o'clock that she finally made her way across the field past Mr Fitzgerald's red tent to the circle of trees. In case they had gone out already, Becky had prepared a message on her best notepaper – yellow with a pink border and bluebells in each corner folded inside a matching envelope. In it she said how sorry she was for being so mean and that she hoped they could forgive her.

In a way, Becky secretly hoped they had gone out because she was still scared of confronting them face to face. She tiptoed in between the poplar trees whose long branches pointing up into the sky were swaying and rustling in a light breeze. It was funny how the trees seemed to whisper, as if telling each other secrets.

The girl hid for a minute behind the same leafy shrub as on the previous evening and listened intently. She could hear no cheery voices this time, all seemed quiet. They must have gone already, she thought, feeling both regret and a sense of relief. Very well, she would leave the note. Hopefully they would appreciate it and not think so ill of her.

There came a strange clinking noise, like the sound of saucepans knocking together. Becky was poised to slip into the campsite but pulled back instantly. Were they still there? She peered through the leaves. She saw nothing. Then that clinking sound came again. It appeared to be from the other side of the tents. Could it be a squirrel or a rabbit perhaps which had discovered their pots and pans and was scurrying about over them?

Then a large piece of tweed reared stiffly up – a tweed cap; a tweed jacket and some tweed trousers. It could only be Mr Fitzgerald! What on earth was he doing there?

If Becky had felt nervous before about seeing the others, she felt a lot more nervous now. Surely that man had no business going to their campsite when they were not around and poking about through their things. Becky felt slightly sick. What was he after?

Whatever it was, he didn't appear able to find it. He clattered about among their pots, pans and kitchen utensils and then stood in the middle of their tents looking all around, seeming puzzled and rather angry.

To Becky's horror, he began to look in between the trees and she realised he would make his way round to her if she stayed in the same place. She jumped up and dashed to the other side.

He rooted through the undergrowth in a full circle, with Becky leaping off each time he approached. She heard him sigh and tut in exasperation. Then to her dismay, she watched as he unzipped one of the tents and went inside.

She shuddered. What kind of person was he to do that? A minute or so later he emerged empty-handed. He then went to the other tent. She heard a scuffling sound as he rifled through bedding and belongings.

'Aah, now what's this?' she overheard him say. Her heart was beating fast. She felt a strong urge to flee, back to the safety of the farmhouse. She felt anger too and a sense of betrayal at this strange man's behaviour – the man whom she had given permission to camp. She carried on watching.

He backed out of the tent and stood up. He had something in his hand but Becky couldn't see what. Mr Fitzgerald fished something out of it. It looked like thick, curled up paper.

'So, this is their little secret is it?' he mumbled under his breath. 'Aah, that it explains it!'

Mr Fitzgerald ceased muttering and appeared deep in concentration, pulling hard at his wispy moustache as he struggled to read what was written on the paper.

Suddenly, he slipped his hand in his pocket and pulled out his mobile phone. Becky could just about see him tapping away at it. He lifted it to his ear. Becky could hardly breathe with excitement and fear. She was desperate to run but determined to stay and find out what he was up to.

'Duncan?' said Mr Fitzgerald. 'Hi, it's me, Malcolm. How are you this morning?'

A tingle ran down Becky's spine. He had been using a false name! He had called himself Andrew Fitzgerald when he spoke to her on the phone, at least as far as she could recall. He certainly didn't call himself Malcolm anyway. Was even his surname Fitzgerald real or was that fake, too?

'Listen, I might need your help pretty soon,' continued "Malcolm". I've got nowhere searching the field east of the lake. Anyway listen, I think I've made a breakthrough.

Those kids I told you about, well they've come across a Saxon parchment written in Old English. Heaven knows how they found it, they must have dug it up before I had a chance.

'Now my knowledge of Old English isn't great but I know enough to get the gist. It appears to be a message to other members of their tribe to seek out the treasure in some nearby tunnels in a sandstone ridge to the east.

'Yes, yes, there are directions to follow, two left turns then enter a big underground cavern of some kind. I can't read the next bit very easily but the hoard is hidden in a natural recess or aperture in the rock behind some sort of "pole". It may mean a stalactite. I can't make out every word but no matter, that should suffice, I think.'

There was a pause while the other person spoke.

'Yes quite so, we need to act fast. I think that is where they have gone today so there isn't a moment to lose. I shall be heading straight over to the tunnels as soon as I've finished talking to you. Now listen, I need you on standby to come over and give me a hand. If there's any treasure to be found the kids may get to it first. If so, I'll need your help intercepting them and with the removal of all items.

'You need to be ready to get over here within 20 minutes of my call. There's no point coming yet. They have no idea I'm on to them and I want to keep it that way for now . . .'

Becky got up and fled. Mr Fitzgerald would soon be ending his call and when he did, he would be going straight over to the caves where the others were. They could be in danger; they might well end up being trapped below ground, with no-one to help them. Then Fitzgerald and his accomplice would spirit away the wealth that rightfully belonged to her struggling parents.

She had to warn the others! Her instinct pulled her back towards the farmhouse but she took no notice. For once, she would show some mettle and do good for a change. Becky ran eastwards to the gap in the hedge that the others had gone through earlier and tore through it.

CHAPTER THIRTEEN

Down the tunnels

BY the time Becky had turned up at their campsite, the other children were long gone of course. They had been up since 6am, breakfasted, got themselves a packed lunch, made sure they had torches with them and headed off.

They went through a gap in the hedge into the adjacent field to the east in which Mr Owen's sheep were grazing, and through into the next field brimming with a swaying crop of dark green maize, seven feet high with slowly ripening cobs of corn. It was far too dense to walk through so they made their way in single file around the edge until they approached the sandstone ridge on the far side.

The land around it was uncultivated. Mr Owen had obviously allowed the area to grow wild since it was clearly unsuited to farming. There were great boulders here and there, and big, swaying willow trees. The sandstone ridge towered above them, dramatic and red. It was a most impressive sight.

It was not immediately apparent where the entrance to the passageways was, assuming it still existed. Shrubs and trees grew thickly against the ridge making it difficult to see any openings in the rock.

Very few people came this way – not even the farmer and his wife and certainly not Becky. It was the sort of place you knew existed but never bothered with.

'It's lovely round here, isn't it?' said Emily, approvingly, 'so wild and untouched by human hand.'

The others agreed. It was an idyllic spot, especially early in the morning with another hot summer's day starting out fresh and gently warm; everywhere bathed in a soft glow. A light breeze ruffled their hair, scented with the spicy vanilla fragrance of bright yellow gorse flowers. A hint of wild honeysuckle hung in the air.

'Is it time for a tea break?' asked David, 'it doesn't look like we're going to find that tunnel entrance. It's obviously long disappeared.'

'Oh come off it David, we've only just arrived. Get searching,' insisted Lou. 'You always give in too easily. We'll find it – and when we do, you can have your tea break.'

David flashed his once-familiar scowl. He never liked it when Lou criticised him. Fair enough, they would keep searching for the mystery tunnel entrance, if she said so.

Eventually, there it was, next to the spot where they had dumped their rucksacks, only partially obscured by a bush. The trouble was, they had fanned out in both directions from there without noticing what was right in front of them.

'It's here!' exclaimed David. 'How could we have missed it!'

'Do you know what?' said Jack. 'It reminds me of the time when we were on holiday at Abersoch and dad parked his car on the road into Pwllheli looking for a camera shop. We got out and scoured the whole town, only to find we'd parked outside it all along.'

They chuckled at that. Lou hadn't been with them then of course, but she could imagine the amused annoyance of their father. He was a good chap, and so was their mother Mrs Johnson. Lou had enjoyed their company too when she'd met the others at Abersoch. They were so much like what proper parents should be – in contrast to her own.

'Ok David, as promised, you can now have your cup of tea, or ginger beer, and then we'll go exploring!' she announced.

Emily took her tea and sipped it, looking nervously at

the dark hole slightly taller than her hewn into the sandstone rock. It brought back memories of the tunnels at Porth Ysgo, memories she would rather forget.

Lou, perceptive as always, noticed her discomfort. 'Hey listen Emily, it will be all right you know. Nothing bad will happen this time, I promise you.'

Emily wasn't easy to comfort. They might not be playing cat and mouse with the smugglers this time but what about that creepy Mr Fitzgerald? Although, as Jack pointed out, how could he possibly know about their interest in the sandstone tunnels?

'I'm sorry,' sobbed Emily. 'I'm sorry but I don't want to go in there. It's too soon. I was scared at Porth Ysgo being held prisoner underground. I can't cope with going back underground again, it wasn't much more than a month ago.'

'Hey listen, don't worry,' said Lou, rubbing her shoulder. 'If you want to stay out here in the sunshine then that's fine. You don't have to come if you don't want to. Here, have this torch – if you change your mind or you need us, come through the entrance and follow the chalk marks we'll leave on the wall. Listen, this is important, I'm not going to leave big long streaks, just occasional dashes and low on the wall so no-one who isn't looking for them will notice them.'

'Are you sure you don't mind?' asked Emily, her soft blue eyes looking sad.

'No, honestly, you guard the entrance!' said Lou. 'Hey, the sun will be striking this sandstone ridge in a few minutes, why don't you sit against it and do a spot of sunbathing?'

That was nice of Lou. She had a knack of making people feel good about themselves which the others appreciated. She was aware, too, that Emily was only 10 and not always confident enough to do the things which came more easily to older children.

In truth, David was feeling somewhat uneasy about entering the tunnel too, but he was determined not to show it. If Jack was to follow Lou, then so would he. Anyway, he couldn't bear the thought of not being there to see the treasure – if any was to be found, of course.

'Come on,' said Lou, flicking on her torch. 'I'll lead the way. We may well have to walk in single file at first. I need to hold the directions from the old parchment. Jack, can you take this piece of chalk and mark the walls as we go? That will ensure we don't get lost. David, you take a torch and shine it around so we can see exactly what we're doing.'

Lou read the directions again to remind herself: '*Down the tunnel, keep straight then left and left again into the cave. Behind the great stalactite high up, is a rock shelf. Up there will ye find what ye seek.*'

'Ok, the easy bit first,' she said – straight ahead until we come to a left turn.'

To their relief, the roof of the tunnel rose as they began walking down it and it widened considerably. The tunnel had been cut from the rich, soft red sandstone of the ridge. As rocks go, it would have been fairly easy to gouge out. The passageway was dry and the air, although musty, was ok to breathe.

Jack took care to make good, distinct chalk marks on the side wall. That was vital to ensure they didn't get lost. On the floor was nothing of interest – but significantly, no clue whatsoever that any other living soul had ever been there.

The passageway seemed to be taking them downwards and the air grew colder. Suddenly, they noticed a clear fork to the left. That must be their left turn! They took it. Lou glanced behind to make sure that Jack was still chalking the wall carefully. He was of course. David was at the rear, flashing his torch about.

The tunnel was not always easy to follow in places. Sometimes they had to bend double and on occasion it would narrow alarmingly. Lou was secretly hoping it wouldn't be too long before they came upon their next left turn.

There it was! Another clear fork to the left. Yes, sure enough, the passageway was opening out and the roof was disappearing. They had reached the cave! Jack sensibly stuck to the rear wall and chalked it so they could easily see how to get out. Otherwise they might lose their sense of direction.

The three of them looked around in awe. It took their breath away. To call it a cave was to do it an injustice. It was a simply magnificent cavern. This was not created by the hand of man but was a natural underground hollow. Lou looked at the rock carefully – the sandstone had given way to hard limestone – a rock which naturally forms great caves, fissures and chasms on its own. It bore strange patterns and glittered slightly in the light of the torch. It was a tremendous sight.

For a few seconds, thoughts of the treasure left the three youngsters. This spectacle was itself a treasure – a gift of Mother Nature. They felt privileged to see it, the more so since few people would ever have done so. The Anglo Saxons had been here of course. The members of the tribe responsible for burying the Staffordshire Hoard and a mysterious second hoard – they had been here, so very long ago, and on such an important mission.

Lou, Jack and David now stood where they would have stood. Was this their refuge, their lair? Their place of sanctuary against enemies? Perhaps they made a home here for a while. Here they entrusted some of their most precious possessions when their previous burial site had become threatened by encroaching water.

Lou flicked her torch at the faces of the others, wanting

to see their reaction.

'I am stunned by this place,' Jack said, simply. 'It is breathtaking beyond words.'

He was trembling slightly and Lou grabbed his arm.

'Are you ok?' she asked.

'Yes,' he replied. 'I'm dumbstruck by it. It's like yesterday, walking into Lichfield cathedral and being engulfed in the splendour of it all. But this is underground, a place no-one ever sees. It makes me shiver somehow.'

'Except us,' she said, giving his arm a squeeze. 'Enjoy the moment, don't be overawed by it.'

Lou broke away and scanned the vast cavern carefully with her torch, from left to right.

'Do you see that, over there?' she whispered, as if it would not be polite to talk loudly in this great hall of Mother Nature. 'It's a stalactite – surely it is the one mentioned on the parchment. Look at it hanging down all that way, like a great stone sausage, almost to the floor. The ledge ought to be somewhere behind it.'

The others walked over the uneven rocky floor towards it. David put his hand out, wishing to touch the stalactite, but Lou pulled him back.

'It's best not to,' she said, softly. 'The oils in human skin can interfere with their formation and change their colour. Let's not damage something that nature has taken hundreds of years to create.'

David withdrew his hand and looked at Lou wondering, not for the first time, how she knew such things. He was considered the brainy one, but in truth, Lou was in many ways far more knowledgeable and able than him.

'Come on, the suspense is killing me, let's find out if the cupboard is bare once and for all,' said Lou. 'If our quest to find the treasure ends here, then let's get it over with.'

She and David flashed their torches around the rock walls behind the stalactite. Jack had a torch too and wanted to use it but sensibly left it safely in his rucksack for now as a useful spare.

Lou saw a distinct void high up in the rock before David but said nothing, wanting him to be the first to spot it.

'Oh I say look, Lou, look up there!' said David. 'Can you see how the rock seems to disappear into blackness. Could that be the shelf?'

'Yes, you're right. Well done David!' she said. 'That's certain to be it – it's a natural shelf about two feet across behind the stalactite. Slight problem, however, is how do we get up there? None of us is tall enough to reach that high.'

Jack and David looked despairingly at Lou. It had never occurred to them that the rocky ledge might simply be out of their reach, although it should have done, since the writing on the parchment said it was 'high up'. Now what were they to do?

'Has anyone got a rope ladder,' said Lou, grinning. 'That might be a start.'

They shook their heads.

'I tell you what, let's use mine, shall we? I've got one which rolls up incredibly small and I brought it on holiday with us in case it might prove handy. Here David, shine your torch on my rucksack and I'll dig it out,' said Lou, as the boys looked on in admiration.

Why could Lou think about such a thing when it never seemed to occur to either of them. They would be lost without her!

'We may not be able to use it, however,' cautioned Lou, as she unravelled it. 'It depends if we can find anything to attach it to.'

The rope ladder had a loop at the top which needed to be hooked over something, but what? For a moment, Lou was at a loss.

Then Jack noticed a large, flat rock in the torchlight.

'Lou, let's get that rock over there and put it up against

the wall,' he said. 'If I lift you up onto my shoulders and use it as a doorstep, you might be able to reach up to the shelf and heave yourself onto it.'

It almost worked. With Lou on Jack's shoulders and Jack standing on the rock she could reach the shelf with her fingertips but she didn't have enough grip to lift herself up onto it.

'David, hand me the rope ladder,' said Lou. 'Now's the time to ask for some luck.'

He gave it her and Lou threw the looped end over the shelf, hoping it would snag on a jutting out piece of rock. If the shelf was anything like the floor of the cavern, then it would have several bumpy, knobbly bits.

Three times she tried with no success but Lou wasn't the sort to give up easily, she tried again, seeking to drag the loop gently over the surface. It snagged! On what exactly, she didn't know but she yanked it downwards as hard as she could and it was fast.

'I'm going up there,' said Lou. 'Do you mind, David? It ought to be you really but I think it should be me who takes the risk of this rope ladder slipping.'

'You go ahead Lou, I don't mind at all. We would never have got this far without you,' replied David.

'Or without Becky!' said Lou with a grin. 'Ok, here goes.'

She grabbed the rope ladder with both hands and gingerly lifted herself onto it. Jack valiantly stood below in the event that it should give way. It didn't and Lou slowly and painstakingly pulled herself up the rungs and onto the shelf. She extracted the torch from her jumper where she'd put it while she needed both hands free.

She flashed it onto the rope ladder. It was perfectly secure, that was a relief. She resisted the temptation to look around the shelf for a moment, although she thought she caught a dull glimmer of something in the torchlight and her heart leapt.

'Hey, listen you two. This rope ladder is perfectly safe. Does it extend to the cave floor? If so, why don't you both come up and we'll shine our torches around the shelf at exactly the same time. Then we can be amazed together, or disappointed together.'

'Yes the rope ladder is plenty long enough. Fantastic, thanks Lou!' shouted up Jack, although David didn't look totally sure he wanted to trust himself to it.

'David, you go up first,' said Jack, kindly, noticing his brother's hesitant face. 'That way I'll be here to catch you if you fall. Try not to though, you big lump!'

David grinned at that. 'Ok,' he said, 'if you don't mind. I promise I won't peek until you're up here too.'

'None of us will, Jack,' called Lou. 'We'll wait for you.'

With some trepidation, David squeezed his torch under his trouser belt and grabbed hold of the rope ladder, pulling himself up and carefully placing his feet on the bottom rungs. He didn't like the way it swayed but soon got the hang of it. Jack got his torch out and shone it upwards to help him. He then scrambled up, quicker and more sure-footed than his brother, and clambered up on to the shelf.

There was actually plenty of room for the three of them. They could just about sit up straight. Jack and David got their torches ready, taking care not to shine them over the shelf until Lou gave the command. They could hardly wait!

CHAPTER FOURTEEN

Underground thriller

IN their hearts, the boys felt almost certain nothing would be there, particularly Jack. From the moment David suggested they go camping in search of a long-lost hoard of Anglo-Saxon treasure which no-one had ever managed to find, he hadn't for one moment seriously expected them to do so.

It had provided the perfect excuse to gang up with Lou again, that was all. For her, it was a chance to get out of the house and be with her new friends. After a few twists and turns their quest had eventually led them here, to a rocky shelf, high up in an underground cave. It was a huge stroke of luck that they had even got this far.

How could they be too disappointed if this was the moment when their luck ran out? Yes of course, after a thousand years, the treasure would be long gone – either spirited away in Anglo-Saxon times by the very tribe to whom it belonged or by others in the centuries since.

Lou, having thought she saw a faint glimmer of something, was slightly more optimistic, but was quite ready to believe it was nothing but wishful thinking on her part.

'I'll count from one to three,' said Lou, 'and then we turn round together and shine our torches down and see what we shall see. If it's nothing, it doesn't matter, it's still been huge fun.

'One, two, three!'

Lou, Jack and David turned to face into the shelf, their powerful torches lighting it up right to the back with a dazzling glare.

They had expected to see nothing and . . .

They were wrong! They were gloriously wrong! David

grabbed Jack's arm and he grabbed Lou's. The three of them held each other tight not daring to believe what was in front of them.

Treasure! Lots of it! Strewn about in one big, messy heap. Much of it was gold, they could tell it was gold. It did not dazzle brightly under the light but smouldered a rich, luxuriant brownish-yellow. The white-grey pieces looked strongly like solid silver, needing just a good polish to bring back their original lustre.

Amidst it all, precious stones, crystal and embedded pieces of coloured glass flickered gently from countless items of exquisite jewellery. The flashes of red might well be garnet – the same precious stone which adorned the brooch from the broken bottle. As their eyes grew used to the flare of the torches and they began to take everything in, they noticed that many of the pieces bore highly complex, ornate designs.

'This is beauty and magic beyond anything I have ever known,' said David, in a low, almost trance-like voice. 'To think it has lain here undiscovered for over a thousand years. To think that the last human hands to touch these wonderful objects were our Anglo-Saxon ancestors, almost as far back in time as the Romans.'

'Yes,' said Jack. 'I can barely believe what I am looking at and I can't put into words how I feel. Hey David, you were right all along!'

'I never expected to find anything either, deep down,' admitted David. 'I certainly didn't expect this. I just thought it would be worth a try.'

'My goodness it was worth a try,' whispered Lou. 'This is worth more than we have any idea of, and not just in money. This will prove an important part of Britain's heritage – missing pieces in the jigsaw puzzle of our history. Let's crawl a bit further in and get a better look. It won't hurt to touch these items will it, David?'

'I shouldn't think so. They're sturdy enough, or they

wouldn't have survived this long. This shelf is bone dry, probably the perfect conditions to preserve them. It might be a good idea to take a photograph of it though in its original state before we touch anything,' he said. 'Erm, having said that, I'm not sure I remembered to bring my little camera.'

'Nor me, I must admit,' said Jack.

'Tell you what, shall we use mine?' said Lou, not for the first time, and they chuckled. Lou pulled a small pocket camera from a side pocket of her rucksack and took several shots. The spectacle in front of them looked even more amazing under a bright flash.

The three of them wriggled alongside the ancient objects and gently lifted two or three pieces up.

'Are we sure this is definitely Anglo Saxon?' said Jack. 'Is this the missing treasure – the items which didn't form part of the Staffordshire Hoard which everybody knows about?'

'From what I know and the pictures that I have seen, I would say so,' replied David. His voice was quiet, David was not one to get excited easily, but Lou saw the delight in his eyes at what they had found.

'You see, these are not the same sort of militaristic items found in the Hoard in 2009. These are more feminine and domestic – brooches, rings, necklaces, belt buckles, fasteners, drinking goblets,' said David. 'Even so, the patterning on them resembles the items from the Hoard. You can imagine them belonging to the same tribe and, for whatever reason, they decided to bury them for safekeeping and split them into two.'

For David, this was a particularly wonderful moment. He had been right all along, even if, typically, he hadn't had much faith in himself. He had spotted the connection between claims in a long-forgotten Victorian book of a second Anglo-Saxon hoard in Staffordshire and a modern book which said that the Staffordshire Hoard was incomplete. He had persuaded the others that it was worth a bash trying to find it and it looked like he had been proven entirely right.

Lou was pleased for him. He deserved this moment. She reached over and gave him a hug and David felt like he could burst with pride.

The three of them fell silent as they spent a while longer gazing at the spectacle in front of them and reverently lifting up a few pieces and imagining what they meant to the people who left them there. What must their lives have been like and what stories could they tell?

'We must not spend too long underground,' said Lou, eventually. 'We must remember that Emily is on her own and might be getting worried about us. We must also decide what we do about this incredible find. My guess is that since Mr Fitzgerald knows nothing about this location we are safe to leave the treasure here for now and it's probably the best place for it until it can be properly handed over to the authorities.'

'In any case, it should be trained archaeologists, not us, who remove it from here,' pointed out David, sensibly.

'Would it be ok to take something with us to show Emily?' said Jack to the others. 'I don't want her to miss out on seeing the treasure.'

Lou didn't reply for a moment. In the torchlight, Jack noticed her stiffen and her sharp eyes to narrow slightly. He knew the signs, and so did David. Lou had an animal's ability to sense danger and seemed to react the same way.

'Keep silent for a minute both of you. Switch off your torches,' she hissed, snapping off hers. 'I think I heard something.'

Lou crawled over to the edge of the shelf. With lights extinguished, everywhere went black. Not for long. Every few seconds a dim shaft of light spilled into the great void below. It caused sparkles in the rocks. Then it disappeared again and went dark. That could mean only one thing:

torchlight! Someone was coming down the tunnel. Who?

'Stay at the back of the shelf and don't make a sound,' Lou instructed the boys. 'Don't switch on your torch whatever you do. It is probably Emily but we can't take any chances.'

The flickers were growing stronger. Suddenly, a burst of torchlight jittered its way across the walls. Then came a familiar voice. Thank goodness, it *was* Emily!

'Jack, David, Lou! Where are you? It's Emily. Oh please, I'm frightened, answer me.'

'Emily, we're up here,' said Lou, flicking on her torch. She shone it down. 'Over here behind that stalactite in front of you.'

Emily gazed up to see Lou's torch shining from up high in the rock face. She put her hand to her mouth. 'How ever did you get up there?' she gasped.

'By rope ladder. Listen Emily, it's great news, we've found the treasure! I'm so pleased you've . . .' and then Lou's voice faltered as she noticed a shadowy figure in the background.

'Emily, who's that behind you?'

'It's Becky,' said Emily. 'I'll explain later. Now Lou, listen to me, I've got bad news. We are in danger and so is whatever you've found. Mr Fitzgerald is on to us. He knows we're in here looking for the treasure and could turn up at any moment. We simply have to get out and quickly.

'That's impossible, how? Was it Becky who told him?' asked Lou, not pausing to consider how Becky would know either. Her voice sounded cold and sharp as it echoed through the cavern. What on earth is she doing here?'

'It was Becky who warned me. She's on our side Lou, trust me on this. We have got to get out of here quickly.'

'How long have we got before Fitzgerald gets here,' said Lou. 'Come on, quickly, think!'

'Not long Lou,' replied Emily, whose face looked worried and had turned a ghostly pallor in the torchlight. 'He raided our campsite and found the parchment. He's managed to work out most of what it says. He'll most probably be going back to his tent to get his torch and some boots and he'll be over here.'

'It will take us quarter of an hour at least to get out of these tunnels and it means leaving the treasure unguarded. We've got no choice. If we stay here, we're trapped,' said Lou. 'And Fitzgerald may not come alone, he may bring friends. We can't take the risk of us being tied up and held prisoner again and this time, I'd be a prisoner too.

'Emily, hold the bottom of the rope ladder as steady as you can and we'll climb down.'

Lou was about to wriggle over the ledge and onto the ladder when something stopped her. She thought she caught yet another glimmer of light from the tunnel!

'Everyone, switch torches off, instantly,' commanded Lou.

She was right! A faint light came from the direction of the tunnel. Lou felt her stomach knotting. This time, that light could mean only one thing: danger.

'We're too late,' whispered Lou to Emily. 'It looks like Fitzgerald is already here. There's only one thing for it, you and Becky are going to have to climb up the rope ladder onto the ledge with us. It's our only hope. Otherwise we are certain to be caught – we probably will be anyway.'

Lou flicked her torch back on. It was a risk but she had to give the girls below enough light to see by. They still had a minute or two while whoever it was found his way along the tunnel. With his own torch on, he shouldn't notice theirs.

Becky did her best to hold the rope ladder steady while Emily tried to climb it. But Emily was trembling too much. This was her worst nightmare coming true – being trapped underground once again with bad people right on their tail. She shivered and shook and the rope ladder simply wouldn't stay still.

Half way up, she lost her footing and fell. Emily was so frightened that the shriek she tried to utter simply wouldn't come out. That was fortunate, since it would have echoed along the tunnel and been heard by whoever was coming up it. She braced herself for a hard, painful fall onto the cave floor. It never came. Becky opened her arms and caught her, toppling back and falling herself as she did so.

She was bruised but not badly hurt. She got up quickly and pulled Emily up with her.

'Here, get on my back Emily,' said Becky, 'you don't weigh that much. Hold on tight and I will climb the rope ladder. Hold me tightly round my shoulders.'

Emily did so, gratefully. She was scared of climbing up to the shelf but petrified of remaining below with someone approaching – and that someone almost certainly being the creepy Mr Fitzgerald.

She clung on tight to Becky who began slowly and painstakingly to ascend the ladder. She wasn't the most physically active of girls and Emily was like a lead weight. But being a couple of years older than the others, plus a combination of adrenaline, fear and the determination to do something right for a change, gave her added strength. With Lou shining a torch along the rungs of the rope ladder she gradually hauled herself up.

Lou shot nervous glances towards the tunnel. The flickering light was getting stronger and stronger. Any moment now the person holding that torch would be in the cave with them and likely spot their light. As Becky neared the top Lou stretched out her hands ready to haul them both onto the shelf.

Suddenly, the flicker from the tunnel became a direct shaft of light. Becky and Emily could see it reflecting off the tunnel walls around them. Lou prayed that the thick stalactite might give them a few extra seconds of cover.

With one final heave and Lou pulling as hard as she could, Becky half flopped over the edge of the rock shelf. As she did so, Lou flicked off her torch and pulled Emily off her back. Relieved of the weight, Becky could pull herself up with relative ease.

Lou hauled up the rope ladder as quickly as she could. The girls crawled on their hands and knees to the back of the shelf where Jack and David had remained. The boys put their hands out to the girls to guide them. There the five of them had to stay, in complete and utter silence and darkness, and pray that they were not discovered.

Yet a chill crept across their hearts. Mr Fitzgerald had got hold of the parchment and had managed to translate it. He had found his way along the tunnel and into the cave. Presumably he had read on far enough to understand that the priceless Anglo-Saxon hoard was on the shelf behind the stalactite. That would be the next place he would shine his torch. He would find both them and the treasure, it was a certainty!

CHAPTER FIFTEEN

In a tight spot

THE children could barely breathe with excitement and fear. It was torture to think that their marvellous find could be snatched from them at any moment, and that they might be in danger themselves.

Their best hope was to lie completely silent and hope none of them sneezed. The slightest noise in that vast, underground chamber would be picked up and bounced off the walls a dozen times. The crucial thing was, did Mr Fitzgerald know that the treasure was on the shelf? If he didn't perhaps a sliver of hope remained.

A powerful torchlight swept across the cave forwards and backwards. Someone was clearly looking hard for something. The five children lay bunched up fearfully watching as what appeared to be a searchlight spilt onto the roof of their rocky ledge and then away again. Every time the beam came towards them they froze, feeling certain it had been spotted.

Round and round, up and down the torchlight swept until it appeared to focus on something. Looking towards the lip of the shelf, Lou could see a halo of light on either side of something dark. The stalactite! The torch was trained on the stalactite! Blow, that was bad news.

'Aah,' came a voice from below. 'What a magnificent stalactite.'

The voice was familiar and chilling. It belonged, without the slightest doubt, to the man who called himself Mr Fitzgerald.

'Now then, there should be a natural recess, an alcove of some kind set into the wall directly behind it,' came his well-spoken, rather pompous voice. Like many older people, he was fond of talking to himself when he thought no-one was listening.

'Hmm,' they heard him say. 'I can't see one.'

The children could see from the shadows springing up on the roof of the shelf, that he was swishing his torch from side to side directly under them.

'How frustrating, I'm sure that's what the parchment said. 'Let's have another look.' Mr Fitzgerald could be heard scrabbling about through his pockets, presumably for the parchment or a copy of it.

'Hmm,' he said again, as if deep in thought. 'Aah, the recess in the wall is . . . blow, I can't read that word. Whatever could it mean? Ah, "high" perhaps?'

Mr Fitzgerald flicked his torch up the wall above his head. He hadn't thought to look right up there. He saw what looked like a dark patch on the cave wall and shone his torch closer.

'Aah,' he said again, maddeningly. 'That must be it – a natural shelf in the rock but rather high I fear. Is there a large stone of some kind I could stand on?'

There was of course – the one which they had found and originally tried to use. They had dragged it out of the way once the rope ladder had been unfurled. They heard a scraping sound as Mr Fitzgerald dragged it back again.

'Hmm,' said Mr Fitzgerald. 'If I stand on that stone will I have enough height to pull myself up? Not quite, unfortunately. Then I could perhaps try climbing up the rock. There look to be a couple of natural footholds.'

The children up above went rigid with fright. Fitzgerald was going to try climbing up? Surely the wall was too sheer for that?

'I'll put my lantern on first, so I can see what I'm doing,' said Fitzgerald to himself.

Its beam radiated out across the walls and created a faint glow on the shelf. The children could now dimly see each other. The treasure offered up a dull gleam. If that creepy man succeeded in peering over the top he would be sure to realise something was up there. The slow wait to be captured was simply torture for the children. They almost felt like giving up.

Lou was worried about the others. She could hold her nerve easily enough and so too, probably, could Jack. She was less certain about David and worried about Emily. In the low light, she looked as if she was shaking. Lou wanted to reach out and give her arm a reassuring squeeze but she dared not, in case it made her jump and cry out.

As for Becky, she was a completely unknown quantity. Lou had no idea how Becky could have known what Mr Fitzgerald's plans were and why she had come to warn them. Quite possibly, she was helping him set a trap for them out of sheer spite, though why she would take things that far she couldn't imagine. Bizarrely, she was now with them, and hiding from him – or pretending to.

Such gloomy thoughts were interrupted by a horrible sight. What looked like two big black spiders appeared over the edge of the shelf. They weren't spiders. They were fingers. Creepy Mr Fitzgerald's fingers! He had succeeded in climbing the wall and now his hands were coming over the top!

Emily was about to scream in terror but then something most unexpected happened. The spidery hands disappeared. The yell came, not from Emily, but from Mr Fitzgerald himself.

There came a dull thud, followed by a clatter and tinkling of shattering glass. It could only mean one thing. Mr Fitzgerald had fallen from the wall and landed in a heap of tweed on the cave floor! The torch he had tucked into his clothing had leapt free and smashed.

'Blast it,' he exclaimed. 'Drat and blast it!'

He pulled his sprawled out limbs up with a groan. 'Oh dear me, that was painful. No bones broken though I don't think.'

Mr Fitzgerald's lantern still worked as he hadn't quite landed on top of it.

'Once more for good luck!' he muttered as he again attempted to scale the wall.

The children groaned inwardly.

It was no good. He was simply too old, stiff and bruised to climb up a second time.

'Drat it, there's nothing for it,' they heard him say, 'I shall have to go and get a ladder from somewhere. Oh blast it, what a nuisance. At least there's no sign of those kids.'

With one final 'drat' and 'blast', Mr Fitzgerald held up his lantern, limped his way gingerly out of the cave and was gone.

As soon as she felt it was safe, Lou flicked on her torch. Emily and Becky gasped at the sight of the treasure. It was the first time they had seen it. There was no time to marvel at it, they had to decide what to do, and quickly.

'We have a choice,' said Lou. 'We can escape this place so we're no longer at risk and abandon this priceless hoard to Mr Fitzgerald, or we can gamble on having at least half an hour or so until he returns and use that time to try to move it to safety. Between us, we only have two big rucksacks to carry it in.'

'I'm willing to give it a shot,' said Jack. 'I can't bear the thought of that man getting his hands on it.'

'Nor me,' said David. 'Let's take a chance.'

'I'd like to help too,' said Becky.

Emily was too frightened to say anything.

'Jack and David, you will help me move the treasure,' commanded Lou. 'Emily and Becky you are to look out for Mr Fitzgerald. If you see any sign of him you need to race back into the tunnels and shout as loud as you can and the rest of us will leg it out of here and escape. Is that understood?'

The others nodded.

'Right,' said Lou, unfurling the rope ladder. 'We will leave the tunnels together to be sure that Fitzgerald has cleared off. We'll then empty as much as we can from our rucksacks and Jack and David will come back with me to start taking everything away.'

Lou was grateful for the chalk marks she had left on the walls. It meant they could get out reasonably quickly. It didn't appear that Mr Fitzgerald had noticed them on his way in – it had been a wise precaution to mark the wall discreetly, and low down. Had he seen them, he would have realised they had got there already.

Would they have enough time to move the treasure? She couldn't say for sure but she was determined to take the risk. She did not know how that strange man had got on their tail so fast, nor could she work out Becky's involvement but he was rotten to the core, she was convinced of it.

As for Becky, she had never felt so unsure about anyone before. If she had betrayed them to Mr Fitzgerald then it was already too late. However, the farm girl appeared to be helping them and they had no choice but to take her on trust, for now at least.

They felt huge relief to step out of the dark tunnels into the bright sunshine. None of them wished for one minute to return – but nor did they wish to leave the horrid Mr Fitzgerald with a free run to loot the place. They were determined to stop him, if they could.

Emily and Becky walked back across the grass, round the maize crop and over to the gap in the hedge. Fitzgerald was sure to take that route upon his return. If they watched out for him there, they should have time to run back through the tunnels and warn the others before he approached, particularly if he was carrying a ladder.

Lou, Jack and David dumped the contents of their rucksacks behind a couple of willow trees, well out of sight. It would also be a good place to hide as much treasure as they had time to recover. They went back into the tunnels taking with them only their torches and empty rucksacks. Lou had left the rope ladder fast and hanging down to the cave floor, awaiting their return.

With little to carry, and chalk marks to follow, the three of them got back to the cave quickly. Lou, who was more nimble and agile than the other two, went up the rope ladder, climbing like a monkey. David came up half way and Lou reached and passed him a full rucksack when she had packed every inch of it with items from the hoard. He then passed it to Jack, waiting on the cave floor.

It was a good system, allowing them to fill the rucksacks easily, without too much climbing up and down the rope ladder. Returning was more cumbersome since the baggage weighed heavily on their shoulders. They emptied out the contents as carefully as they could and then went back to load up again.

The three of them made four journeys to and from the underground cave. They returned for what they guessed would be their final time. Forty minutes had passed however and Lou was getting nervous. They had gone beyond the half-hour limit they had set. Mr Fitzgerald might well be back at any time and common sense told her that they should abandon the few remaining items that were left.

None of them could bear the thought of Fitzgerald having so much as a coat button from that hoard. He didn't deserve to get his greedy fingers on any of it. So they carried on, determined not to leave a thing.

They were half way through loading up when they heard Emily's desperate cries echoing through the tunnel.

'Get out, get out quickly! Hurry! He's coming back!'

Lou hurled the last few items into the rucksack and swept her torch quickly around the shelf. Nothing was left. They had taken every last piece. She got down the rope ladder as quickly as she could. Then it occurred to her that the rope ladder was held fast to the top of the shelf! She pulled herself back up again and released it, and threw it to Jack and David.

'Listen you pair, I'm going to ease myself over the shelf as far as I can until I'm holding on by my fingertips,' said Lou. 'You need to grab my legs and help me fall gently.'

They did so and she made a relatively safe landing on the floor of the cave. She bundled up the rope ladder into her rucksack as quickly as she could.

'Now let's run! As fast as we possibly can!' she cried. They did so, stumbling at times and nearly falling flat on their faces. They had to pray that they had left themselves enough time before Mr Fitzgerald turned up with his ladder.

As they got to the exit, Lou peeped out to see if they were safe to slink out. To her horror, she saw Becky chatting to Mr Fitzgerald on the far side of the field. So Becky was in league with him! She must have betrayed them!

CHAPTER SIXTEEN

Cat and mouse

'GET down the pair of you!' snapped Lou. 'Fitzgerald is over there and he could easily see us. We're going to have to crawl on our tummies and hope he doesn't spot us.'

Fortunately, Becky was standing in such a way that Mr Fitzgerald could not easily see the tunnel entrance – at least not the bottom half of it. Lou, Jack and David wriggled like worms out into the longer grass. They kept wriggling until they were under the cover of shrubs and rocks and then made their way slowly to their hiding place.

Having got out of the tunnel a minute or so before them, Emily slipped through the long grass, keeping as low as she could and crawled as near to Becky as she dared, trying to catch her eye. Eventually, Becky shot a nervous glance around her and Emily bobbed up and gave her a thumbs up then disappeared out of sight.

'Right,' said Becky, understanding the signal. 'Well it's been lovely talking to you Mr Fitzgerald. Good luck with your bat spotting. Are you sure you don't want a hand with that ladder?'

'Quite sure,' replied Mr Fitzgerald. 'Nice talking to you. Do give my regards to my fellow campers when you see them. Gone off to Lichfield for the day shopping, you say? How nice for them. Anyway so long as they're all right – I popped over to their campsite earlier to check on their welfare and was puzzled I couldn't find them anywhere. I worry for them you know, they're so young.'

'Well if I see them I'll tell them to pop round and let you know that they're ok,' said Becky, flashing a smile as false as one of Mr Fitzgerald's. 'I wouldn't worry too much though, I'm sure a brassy, pushy lot like them know how to take care of themselves. The less I see of them the better, quite frankly.'

'Yes, I'd rather picked up on the fact that you didn't get along awfully well with them,' said Mr Fitzgerald. 'I have to say they've been somewhat cold and stand-offish with me as well. It's certainly a much more pleasant experience talking with a charming young lady like yourself.'

'Oh you're too kind, Mr Fitzgerald, thank you,' said Becky, rewarding his oily compliment with another insincere smile. 'Bye for now.'

'Yes, goodbye for now, Becky.'

With that, Mr Fitzgerald, or whatever his real name was, marched stiffly off heading for the tunnels, a big, empty rucksack over his tweed shoulders and a light aluminium ladder under his arm. He was limping slightly after his rather painful fall that morning.

Lou had been staring mutely and angrily at the pair of them as they chatted. When Mr Fitzgerald disappeared she was surprised to see Emily suddenly pop up and rejoin Becky. Lou stepped out from behind the willow trees with Jack and David following and marched straight up to them both.

'Right, you listen to me,' said Lou, her cat-like green eyes flashing with suspicion and anger at Becky. 'I want straight answers from you. What is going on? Have you betrayed us to that crook Mr Fitzgerald? If so, you're an even bigger fool than I took you for.'

Becky looked at Lou, and then at Emily, and back at Lou again. Her big brown eyes were not filled with loathing and scorn this time but meekness and sorrow, or something approaching it.

'I *am* a fool Lou,' said Becky, quietly. 'I deserve you to think badly of me. But I'm not on his side, not at all. I'm on yours. I am truly sorry for my awful behaviour over the last few days. The least I can do to make it up to you is to help you.'

Lou looked hard into her eyes, determined to decide once and for all whether Becky was good at heart or rotten. She still couldn't be sure.

'I don't understand,' said Lou, in a slightly softer tone. 'It sounds too good to be true. I need to know what's going on Becky. You've been horrible to us over the last few days, especially to me. You know we've got the treasure out of that cave. It belongs to your parents, far more than it belongs to us. Above all, it doesn't belong to Mr Fitzgerald and we do not intend him to get a single piece of it. Have you betrayed us to him, yes or no?'

'Erm Lou, can I say something,' said Emily, timidly. 'It was Becky who came and found me while you were down the tunnels to warn me that Mr Fitzgerald was on to us and that you were in danger.'

'Right,' said Lou, sharply again. 'This is what I don't understand. How did Becky know that we were seeking the treasure in the sandstone tunnels on this farm and above all, how did she also know that Mr Fitzgerald had found out that we were on to it and was coming after us?'

'I can explain everything,' said Becky, 'just give me a chance.'

'Well be quick,' said Lou, glancing at the tunnel entrance. 'It won't take Mr Fitzgerald long to discover that the underground shelf is now bare. He will come out in a furious temper and he'll be wondering where we are and what we're up to. So we need to know whose side you're on and fast.'

'I went over to your campsite yesterday evening to apologise to you all for the way I'd acted,' explained Becky, 'particularly to you, Lou, for knocking you over. I felt terrible about it and I wanted to say sorry. When I got into the circle of trees around your little camp I realised you were about to eat and I didn't want to disturb you. I couldn't help but overhear your conversation.

'You said some mean things about me which I know I deserved but because you were so angry with me, I lost my nerve and didn't have it in me to burst in and apologise. So I waited a while and I overheard you talking about the parchment you found and the translation you got from the priest at the cathedral, and how it had led you to believe the treasure might be inside the underground tunnels and that you were going to visit them today for a look.

'At that point I ran away, back to the farmhouse. I came back this morning hoping to catch you before you left to say sorry. The trouble is, I overslept and then spent a bit of time getting ready – you know, showering and washing my hair – and by the time I got there, you'd gone.

'I had already written you a note to apologise in case I'd missed you, which I planned to leave at your campsite. I have it here look, in my pocket.'

Becky pulled out the note and gave it to Lou.

'Just as I was about to step through the trees I heard a noise – at first I thought you must still be there but then to my horror I could see the back of a man dressed in tweed. I knew instantly it was Mr Fitzgerald,' she continued.

'I couldn't understand why he was in your campsite when you weren't there and then he went into your tents and searched through them. In one of them he must have found the parchment because he was examining it and he took a photo of it with his camera.'

Lou, Jack and David listened wide-eyed in astonishment and disgust.

'I had that parchment kept safe in the broken bottle under my pillow,' exclaimed Lou. 'How dare that creepy man rifle through our personal things in that way? Not for one minute did I think he would stoop to doing that!'

'Anyway, his real name may well not be Mr Fitzgerald,' went on Becky, quietly. He phoned somebody, a mate of his presumably, to tell them of his discovery, and he called himself Malcolm. When I first spoke to him on the phone and took his booking, he had called himself Andrew Fitzgerald.'

'That's right,' said Jack. 'He called himself "Andrew Fitzgerald" when we first met him.'

'I overheard him on the phone saying he could work out most of what the parchment said, which was that the treasure had been moved to an underground cave and he was going to get off there,' went on Becky.

'I guessed that's where you'd be and I ran off to warn you and I came across Emily outside and I told her. Fortunately she believed me and the pair of us went into the tunnels together to alert you.'

'If it hadn't been for Becky I'm not sure I would have had the courage to go into those underground tunnels,' admitted Emily. 'Then look how she caught me when I fell and lifted me up onto the shelf.'

'How come she was chatting to Mr Fitzgerald as we came out of the tunnels with the last pieces of treasure?' chipped in Jack, anxious to show that he was as sceptical as Lou about Becky.

'Why do you think, silly,' said Emily, determined to defend Becky. 'You were taking too long in there and we were both worried you wouldn't get out in time. Becky went to chat to him before he got too close in order to delay him.

'Oh come on, Lou, give her a chance, she's saved the day several times over and she's said how sorry she is for the way she's behaved,' added Emily, her soft blue eyes looking imploringly at her.

Lou's eyes were looking hard into Becky's trying once and for all to work her out. Becky held her gaze, and Lou could see no malice in her.

'Come here,' said Lou finally to Becky. She gave her a hug. 'I believe you, let's put what's happened behind us.

Thanks for what you've done today. You're one of us now, ok?'

Becky burst into tears at Lou's sudden and unexpected kindness.

'Hey, dry your eyes, or your make-up will run,' said Lou, with a grin.

Becky laughed. They all laughed. At a stroke the tension had gone. Becky had been accepted by Lou and that was good enough for the rest of them. Now they were friends together – with one common enemy, an unpleasant, dishonest man using the false name of Andrew Fitzgerald.

'We have to decide what to do,' said Lou. 'Let's talk about this over a cup of tea if there is any left in those flasks we brought. It might not be very hot now but it's better than nothing.'

There was some left and it was warm enough. They sat in the long grass drinking their tea out of paper cups and nibbling some chocolate Emily that had thoughtfully brought with them. It was a welcome and invigorating break.

They looked about them. The sandstone ridge was turning a deepening red under the sun which was slowly beginning its descent towards the western horizon. The willow trees under which they had taken cover were casting longer shadows.

Lou glanced at her watch. It was already 4pm. Mr Fitzgerald had been gone about half an hour. He would surely be out any minute. Nothing could be done but wait and hope he came nowhere near them. It would be far too much of a risk to try to move the treasure again and in any case, move it where? Certainly not to their campsite.

They covered the Anglo-Saxon hoard as best they could with handfuls of vegetation, twigs and fallen leaves. It would be difficult to spot unless you were actually looking for it.

The tunnel entrance was a couple of dozen yards away from their hiding place behind the willow trees and several assorted shrubs, including a spiky gorse bush. Mr Fitzgerald would have no reason whatsoever to suspect they were there. With a ladder under his arm, bruised limbs and no doubt in a furious temper, he would most likely simply limp his way back to his little red tent.

So it proved. Lou and Jack were keeping watch on the tunnel entrance through the branches of a willow tree.

'He's coming out,' hissed Lou to the others. 'Keep quiet everybody and stay still.'

Mr Fitzgerald wasn't wearing his trademark tweed cap and his hair looked dishevelled and unkempt. His face appeared red rather than its usual pallor and his greasy thin lips were grimacing into an unpleasant scowl. He didn't look happy at all.

'Drat it,' they heard him say, as he stomped off across the field. He didn't glance once in their direction. They and the treasure were safe – for now at least.

'Becky,' said Lou. 'What did I hear you say to Mr Creepy earlier – something about going bat hunting in the underground caves?'

The others giggled at Lou dubbing him 'Mr Creepy' – it was a good name for him, particularly as the one they knew him by was almost certainly false. From that moment on, Mr Creepy, or plain 'Creepy' was what they would usually call him.

'Yes that's right,' said Becky. 'That's what he needed the ladder for apparently, he wanted to climb up and watch the bats roosting. Maybe he didn't come across any and that's why he doesn't look happy.'

The others chuckled at Becky's little joke and she felt pleased and accepted by them. She felt proud of what she had achieved that day.

'Erm Lou,' said Becky, hesitantly. 'Now that Mr

Creepy has gone, might I have a peek at the treasure?'

'Yes of course,' said Lou. 'You too, Emily, I'm sorry, with all that has happened I had forgotten you hadn't seen it properly.'

The two girls hesitantly picked up a few of the artefacts, marvelling at the intricate designs traced into solid gold and silver. Lou, Jack and David looked on too, interested to see the hoard in natural light. It was a truly magnificent collection and none of them even dared to guess what it might be worth.

'Ok,' said Lou after a while, anxious to get on with things. 'We need to decide now what our next move is. We mustn't under-estimate Mr Creepy. He clearly has an accomplice of some kind who he can phone at any time and bring over here to help him. This treasure still isn't safe – nor are we.'

'What do you propose we should do, Lou?' asked David. 'Do you know what worries me? I don't think it would be safe to take the treasure back to our campsite. In fact, I'm not convinced that we are safe at our campsite ourselves any more.'

David felt particularly protective over the treasure since the whole quest to find it had started with him. He felt a strange affinity to it and indeed, in a funny way, the Anglo Saxons to whom it belonged.

Emily shivered a little. David was right, their campsite amid the trees no longer seemed so welcoming. It was horrible to think that the vile Mr Creepy had gone through their things – even poking around in their tents. It made her feel unclean somehow.

'I have to say I think you're right,' said Lou. 'Mr Creepy's next move will be to look out for our return and hope that we bring back the treasure with us. He now knows that it has gone from the caves and he will suspect that we have found it and taken it away. In which case, he is bound to want to find a way of taking it from us.'

'And having already found the Anglo-Saxon bottle and parchment inside our tent, he'll probably think that anything we manage to find, we'll take back to the campsite with us and hide,' said Jack.

'Which means,' said Lou, 'that our campsite is probably not safe to sleep in and certainly not safe to keep the treasure in. Does everyone agree?'

They nodded but Emily looked scared. The prospect of night falling with Creepy on the prowl and nowhere to sleep was worrying her.

'Perhaps this is getting too much and we should let Becky's parents know and ask them to help us take it away,' Emily said. 'Or maybe let the museum people know and they could come here and get it.'

'I don't think we should be tempted to rush into doing either of those things,' said Lou, standing up and pacing around.

She turned round to face them and spoke quietly but determinedly. 'To involve Becky's parents at this stage with Mr Creepy and possibly his accomplice to deal with would be to ask them to share our danger. That is unfair. Finding this treasure and recovering it safely was our quest. It is we who should finish the task, and Creepy will be on the look-out for anything out of the ordinary.

'If grown-ups are involved, particularly once the museum people get called in, there will be a huge fuss with any number of people coming to and fro photographing everything and making notes, and possibly journalists, too. In the midst of it all, we'll be a bunch of kids trying hard to explain how we managed to translate an Old English parchment which led us to an underground cave and to the treasure.

'Most likely, Mr Creepy will stroll up and take the credit – and lay claim to the whole lot. He'll say it was he who found it, not us and because he's a grown-up, they'll believe him, especially if he can actually translate that parchment himself. Then he will be considered the legal finder and possibly get at least half the value of the treasure.

'So our best hope is to get it to a place of complete safety well away from Creepy without anyone knowing a thing,' continued Lou, 'and then tell Becky's parents and get it reported to the authorities when the moment is right. It would be best to move the hoard under cover of darkness and to do so tonight. The question is, where?'

The others looked up at Lou with respect bordering on awe, including Becky. Lou was the unquestioned leader of the pack. Becky felt miserably embarrassed at how she had treated her the day before. She badly wanted to make amends. As her thoughts strayed to the incident in the farmyard the previous day, Becky suddenly had an idea.

'Hey Lou, what about using one of our big barns? One of them is half full of bales of hay, all stacked up. If we took the treasure there, we could easily lift up a couple of them to create a wide hole, put everything inside and put the bales back on top. It would all be perfectly safe in the hay and completely hidden,' said Becky.

'Then, when we're done, we can sleep the rest of the night in the barn on a comfy bed of hay. I'll tell my parents I'm out camping with you lot tonight so they won't worry. They'll be pleased to think we've become friends.'

'Brilliant!' said Lou. 'That's a wonderful idea, Becky. Is it possible for us to get back to the farmyard from here without having to cross the camping field? Creepy may well not be doing too much sleeping tonight either.'

'Yes,' said Becky, 'this eastern field has a gate at the bottom – we go straight through that, into the field with a few sheep in, through that and we're into the farmyard. I'll be with you to show you the way to the barn and I know how to get into it, of course.'

The others looked at Becky gratefully. She wasn't such

a bad egg after all. With some effort and a lot less make-up she might make a good egg. Certainly she was proving a big help in their efforts to outwit Mr Creepy.

As the shadows lengthened further and the sun tumbled westwards, the children huddled together for warmth. It was getting chillier now and it was, of course, nearly September.

Becky nipped back to tell her parents she had joined the others camping. They were pleased, as she expected. She asked if she could take back some bread and cheese as the others were running low on supplies. There was, of course, plenty of such fare to be had on a farm!

When she returned, Lou and the others were getting peckish. They were delighted to learn that Becky had come armed with a scratch supper!

It was a beautiful evening. The setting sun had transformed into a lovely golden orb which turned the swaying grasses on this wild, uncultivated part of the farm a delightfully rich colour. The sandstone ridge was a dark red. They nibbled their bread and cheese and sipped what remained of the tea, which wasn't very warm now. The five of them felt relaxed and content but excited too.

So far, things were working out well. They had found the most astonishing and historic hoard of centuries-old treasure and managed to whisk it away minutes before it was seized by the spidery hands of an old villain. They were winning!

CHAPTER SEVENTEEN

Night-time challenge

THE five children watched the sun disappear below the horizon. It would not be dark for a good while yet. It was only 8pm. They would not be safe to start moving the treasure for at least another two hours.

It was exciting, nerve-wracking, fun and frightening rolled into one. Lou was at her best in such a situation – with an animal-like alertness and awareness of all around her. Sometimes her fringe of dark hair seemed to cover her vivid green eyes but they saw everything – behind as well as in front. She didn't miss a thing.

As for Becky, Lou was reasonably satisfied that she was a good sort after all. She had been good for them that day. They could not have got where they had without her. Several times she had come to their rescue. Beneath the make-up and the pouting, scowling, vain face was possibly a decent, sensitive soul.

Tonight Becky would have the chance to prove her worth. Lou hoped that her trust would not be misplaced.

As the light faded and little moths began fluttering around the bushes, David, Emily and Becky laid their heads on their rucksacks for a light snooze. They were already tired after an action-packed day and aware that there would be more to come overnight. None of them expected to get much, if any, sleep.

Lou simply sat on the grass, watching and waiting. She couldn't help but feel that this was the calm before the storm; that Mr Creepy might have one more trick up his sleeve to play. Doubtless, he was an intelligent and determined man – and possibly a dangerous one. The worst thing they could do was to under-estimate him and relax. The treasure was now in their possession, but that made them all the more of a target.

Jack came up and sat alongside her. He didn't feel like snoozing and anyway, he wanted to show Lou that he could be as alert and responsible as her. The sky darkened as they sat together, saying little, watching and waiting. Tiny stars began to appear, then more and more, pricking the navy blue sky. They were far brighter than children in towns would ever see them.

'It's one of the great things about living in the countryside,' said Lou, 'being able to see the night sky as it should look – full of the most brilliant stars. In towns, all the lights left on overnight ruin that wonderful view.'

Jack nodded in agreement. He had never stayed in a town overnight but he was sure that was true.

Ten o'clock came and went and Lou decided to let the others sleep a while longer. It still wasn't completely dark although with a half-moon now rising, there would be a little natural light. That was a good thing, since it would be too dangerous to shine a torch.

'Right Jack,' said Lou, when her watch ticked round to 11pm. 'You wake up your brother and sister and I'll give Becky a shake. I've been wanting to give her a shake for a while!'

They both chuckled. Privately, Jack was astonished Lou hadn't thrown her into the lake by now. He thought she had been very forgiving of her. The two of them roused the others who sat up groggily.

As quietly as they could, they began the task of filling their rucksacks with the precious objects, their fingers trembling as they did so. It didn't seem right somehow, to manhandle them in this way, but it was the best option in the circumstances.

Becky had brought back with her a big sports bag as well as her rucksack, both of which she had filled with straw from the farm. That was useful, it allowed the children to pack the items carefully, without banging them and avoiding any giveaway clinks and clatters. For all they knew, the big ears of Mr Creepy might be flapping away behind a nearby tree or shrub, listening to their every move. They had to move in complete silence.

Lou estimated they would need to make about four journeys to get the hoard transferred to the safety of the barn. Then, they could make themselves a bed of hay until the morning. That would be fun!

They staggered their way southwards across the field towards the farmhouse. Fortunately, it was pasture, recently used for grazing cattle. They could dimly see the gate in the moonlight. They went through it into another field, where a flock of sheep were grazing. The animals looked up in astonishment at the sight of the children. Two or three skittered off and a couple began to baa rather plaintively.

'We'll be fine,' whispered Becky. 'Don't worry about them. But let's keep away from the geese if we can, they will quack their heads off if they see us.'

Now she tells us, thought Lou, annoyed that such a possibility hadn't crossed her mind. Another thought struck her – the farmer and his wife. Might they still be up? It was only just gone 11pm. She asked Becky.

'Oh goodness no, don't worry about that,' whispered Becky. They're like all farmers – early to bed, early to rise. There's milking to be done and all sorts of jobs from 4.30 in the morning.'

The children found the first journey to the farmyard hard work. They had filled every last inch of baggage with Anglo-Saxon treasure. It had seemed a good idea at the time but they found it a great struggle to carry it all. Precious metals like gold and silver were surprisingly heavy.

'We'll take less from now on and make more journeys,' panted Lou.

When they staggered gratefully into the farmyard, they hit a snag. There were several barns and in the dark, Becky realised that she wasn't sure which was the one filled with hay.

'I'm sorry Lou, but I'm going to need to flick a torch round ever so quickly,' said Becky, regretfully. She had been anxious not to get anything wrong and to carry on being as helpful as possible. It had not occurred to her that in darkness, one barn looks much the same as another. She hoped Lou would not be cross.

'Ok, don't worry,' said Lou, although she wasn't happy about it. 'Hay barns will have pieces of straw sticking out through gaps in the walls most likely. Let's find it quickly.'

Lou took out her torch and switched it on, praying she would not end up regretting that decision, and they began to walk around the farmyard flicking its powerful light over the outbuildings.

'I think it's that one over there,' said Becky.

Lou stepped round the other side of it, seeking to prevent the torchlight from shining elsewhere in the farmyard and waking the livestock.

'Aah yes,' said Becky. 'that's the one – you're right Lou, there are bits of straw sticking out through the corrugated iron. I remember now, it's the oldest, most rickety barn of the lot. The door hinges are almost rotten through. Can you shine the torch again quickly so I can see where the bolts are?'

Lou pointed the torch at the stable door and Becky drew the bolts back. They were stiff and scraped noisily. She swung the door open on its dodgy hinges and, sure enough, there were neatly-stacked bales of rich, sweet-smelling golden hay.

Some of it was nearly up to the roof. Emily recoiled and gasped as they went inside at what looked like a big pair of gleaming, close-set eyes in the corner. It was only a tractor. She told herself not to be so silly.

They clambered onto the lower reaches of the haystack and lifted up two adjoining bales, then carefully unloaded the treasure into the gap. It had been a great idea of Becky's, this was the perfect place for it. They then put the bales they'd removed back over the top.

'We'll have to be careful we remember which bale we're hiding it under, otherwise it will be like looking for a needle in a, erm, haystack,' whispered David, not intending to be funny.

'You're right David, we'll have to be careful,' said Lou, looking around for something to indicate the right bale.

'Here,' said Becky, 'pitchfork marks the spot!'

'Good,' said Lou, 'now as we leave the farmyard, let's make sure we remember exactly where the hay barn is.'

'Ouch, what was that?' cried David, tripping clumsily over something in the dark.

It was a goose which had spotted the torchlight and waddled over to see what was going on. It quacked noisily and hissed at David, its beak wide open. Several other geese wandered over too and began quacking at him. He backed away hastily, reversing into another goose. He had always been wary of large birds ever since a seagull had landed on his tummy at Abersoch, mistaking it for a rock.

'Come on, let's get out of here,' said Lou.

She flicked the torch on again to see at a glance the speediest way out of the farmyard. The five of them disappeared as quickly as they could into the welcome blackness of the fields. Fortunately the gaggle of geese didn't follow but continued to give the occasional angry quack. Fancy disturbing them in the middle of the night when they were fast asleep. No wonder they were cross!

Without the burden of heavily-laden baggage, the children were able to get back much more quickly. Lou had taken the precaution of leaving a white T shirt hanging on a shrub so they could locate their hiding place more easily. That too was a risk but better than having to put torches on to search for it.

'Ok,' said Lou, when they got back. 'Let's load up again but leave it about 10 minutes or so before we return, to give those geese a chance to get back to sleep.'

She listened intently and looked about her. To her relief she could see and hear nothing. It looked like there was no harm done.

~~~~~

Mr Fitzgerald – or Mr Creepy, as the children now preferred to call him – sat cross-legged in his small tent reading and re-reading the parchment he had stolen from under Lou's pillow, trying his best to make sense of it. His torch was broken of course, but he could just about see under the dim light of his lamp which lit up his face and greasy lips in a particularly unflattering way.

Had he made a mistake translating it? Or was it that he had searched in exactly the right spot only the treasure had long since been plundered? Certainly the old Victorian book on antiquities that Mrs Johnson had so kindly posted to him seemed quite positive that the Anglo-Saxon treasure had originally been buried in two piles – one of which had turned out to be the Staffordshire Hoard.

The other was the field east of the lake in the parish of Wall, down the road. The Victorian experts had clearly been unable to locate either and gloomily assumed both had long gone. It must have been a tough old job, treasure hunting in the days before metal detectors.

They had been wrong about the one hoard and might well have been wrong about the other. Yet how maddening that a bunch of kids had cleverly drawn the same conclusion and might have beaten him to it. He had been
~~~~~

researching the missing Anglo-Saxon treasure since before they were born!

The bizarre twist had been the discovery of the bottle containing the parchment, giving directions to the new location for the missing hoard. It had unquestionably not been touched by another human hand until the kids had found it and broken into it.

Creepy read the parchment again, for the umpteenth time. It was quite clear – the hoard had been moved to a natural shelf high up in the cavern accessed via a tunnel through the sandstone ridge. He had found that shelf and eventually, with the help of a ladder, had got up there to claim it. There was not a trace of it.

For all he knew, that treasure might have been long gone by the time of the Norman Invasion, or pinched as William Shakespeare penned his first play or when man landed on the moon. Or, it might have been whisked off that day by those maddening children, minutes before he got there – assuming they had found someone to translate Old English. Was that why they had disappeared to Lichfield?

Where were they now?, he wondered. He hadn't seen so much as a hair of their heads all day. Well no matter. Their tents were still up and they would be sure to have returned before nightfall. If they had the treasure they would almost certainly keep it close, most likely hidden inside their campsite. One thing was for sure – if they got their hands on so much as a golden goblet, he would wrest it off them, by fair means or foul.

Creepy glanced at his watch. It was a quarter to eleven. He would wait another half hour or so to allow them plenty of time to fall asleep before tiptoeing out to their campsite and taking a good look. If they were sound asleep he might even take a peek inside their tents, or at least under the flysheet.

He was getting sleepy himself. He'd had a long and

frustrating day and his legs and side felt bruised and sore from his fall 'in the underground cave. He stretched himself out on his bedding. There was no rush and after all, the later he left it the more deeply asleep they should be. He settled himself down for a light nap.

About half an hour later, a strange noise awoke him. It was the distant quacking of geese or ducks. They were making a right old din. Crikey I must have over-slept, thought Creepy! Is it morning already?

He staggered to his knees and unzipped the tent flap. It was dark of course. Creepy got up and went outside. How strange! The farmyard geese didn't normally make such a racket overnight. Something must have disturbed them, a fox perhaps. He glanced towards the farmhouse but it was in darkness.

Then he saw a burst of light. It was a straight beam but it jumped about for a second or two then swept briefly up the fields before vanishing. Creepy looked hard towards the farmyard. The light did not reappear.

It was odd, like a flash of torchlight which somebody wanted to switch off as quickly as possible. Was someone lurking about the farmyard and if so, why? Creepy felt a slight shiver down his back. Farms were sometimes targeted at night by rustlers, after all pedigree cattle could be worth thousands. Yet was there a chance that those children were up to something under cover of darkness?

Creepy pulled on his boots and a light jacket and headed off silently towards the farmyard. He walked around the edge of the field rather than straight across it in case he accidentally bumped into them. Surely though, they wouldn't be out and about at this hour? If they were, then they had something to hide – something interesting to hide.

All seemed quiet on the farm. A barn owl hooted, appropriately enough, from a barn roof, but that was all. No-one seemed to be about. Creepy decided to head back across the field but for a brief second he thought he caught the sound of voices, ever so soft and whispering, carried by a light breeze over the flat farmland. Children's voices perhaps? Silence again.

Creepy looked around for a good hiding place. The huge silo – a cylindrical steel tower where animal feed was stored, cast long shadows in the moonlight. He hid behind it and waited.

Several minutes passed. The farmyard was silent. The geese made no sound, and the barn owl must have either put his head under his wing or be out somewhere pouncing on mice. Then suddenly, without warning, Creepy saw dim blobs appear in the weak light of the moon. There were five blobs moving noiselessly across the farmyard.

He heard the slightest creak as if a rather old barn door was opening. Creepy sneaked out from behind the silo, keeping in the shadows. Yes! A narrow streak of light! Whoever it was must have gone into a barn and left the door slightly ajar. He crept closer and listened intently.

Was that some sort of bag being unzipped? Then a metallic clink, he was sure of it. How strange. Whatever was going on?, thought Creepy, his thin, greasy lips puckering into a hint of a smile. He could guess of course. Oh yes, he could guess all right. Those infuriating children. They must have found the treasure! Instead of keeping it in their campsite where he would seize it from them, they were smart enough to hide it in the farm's haystack!

Only they weren't quite smart enough for Doctor Malcolm Finchfield, antique dealer and historian. He would wait patiently until they had carefully deposited every last priceless artefact into a soft bed of hay. Then, when they tiptoed back to their tents for a well-deserved snooze he would get his friend Duncan to drive over in the van they used for their antiques business, load everything into the back of it and they would be away!

Wouldn't the children get a shock when they discovered it had all gone! He, Dr Finchfield, would hand over some of it as the official finder to great acclaim and be paid a fortune by the British Museum as a reward for doing so. He would declare that it was he who had found the hoard, fair and square. Who would believe a bunch of pesky kids over someone of his calibre – an academic, linguist and antiques expert? As for the rest of it, he would dispose of in other, even more lucrative ways.

Dr Finchfield, or Mr Creepy as he was not so fondly known by the children from whom he hoped to steal, smiled gruesomely to himself and grimaced smugly. Soon, he could quit trying to scrape a living in the antiques business and retire. He would be rich!

He padded round the side of the barn while he waited for them to come out. A few minutes later, the creak of the barn door told him they had gone. He hung back a minute or two more, to be sure. Then he tiptoed round and gently pulled the door open. They had left it slightly ajar which presumably meant they had more treasure to bring. It was important he didn't start taking it away before they had finished.

Creepy tiptoed inside. It was dark of course, and he couldn't see a thing. He didn't have a torch on him either, of course. Blow and drat! Aah, but he had his mobile phone which had a bright orange backlight. He pulled it from his pocket and switched it on. It emitted just enough light for him to see that it was indeed a barn full of hay, with what looked like some sort of farm machinery in the corner.

The question was, where exactly was their hiding place? Under a hay bale presumably. He noted that some were stacked to the barn roof while others were more accessible. It was hard to see using only the weak light of his mobile which would switch off after a few seconds.

'Aah,' muttered Creepy, under his breath. A pitchfork was slung over one of the bales. He climbed up, moved it aside and yanked the bale up. He jabbed his mobile to make the backlight come on again and shone it downwards.

There! Treasure, gleaming softly in the weak amber light. Creepy recognised it instantly as an Anglo-Saxon marvel, rippling with superb craftsmanship: pendants, brooches, bracelets, belt buckles, dress fasteners, adorned with the most intricately engraved motifs. The precious stone garnet, much loved by the Anglo Saxons, smouldered red, set in the most carefully crafted gold finery. This was indeed the sister to the great, world-famous Staffordshire Hoard and possibly as valuable.

Creepy pulled the hay bale back over the top and laid the pitchfork across it. He mustn't be tempted to spend too long admiring it. The kids would return soon. He climbed back onto the barn floor and then walked round the rear of the haystack. He made himself a hole amid the bales and curled up in it like a dog in a basket. It was the perfect hiding place and a lot more relaxing than crouching by the side of the silo. He could wait in comfort for them to come and go with more treasure. Then, when they'd cleared off, he would summon Duncan to help him take every last precious item.

Come to think of it, mused Creepy, his mouth snickering into a lopsided grin, they could even take some of the hay, it would make perfect bedding material for safe transportation.

The barn door began to creak. The children must be back with more loot! He could just about hear them the other side of the haystack gently placing more artefacts on top of the others. He hoped they would be careful, it wouldn't do to damage any of it. Was that the last delivery or was there more to come?

'One more trip will do it, I should think,' whispered Lou to the others as they departed.

Fair enough, thought Creepy. There was already enough value in what they had brought to the barn so far for him never to need to work again. Oh such a blessing! No more trailing off across the countryside to antiques fairs in the rain. No more maddening browsers in his shop. Browsers were the bane of antique dealers like Mr Creepy. They would look and point and go 'ooh, takes you back, doesn't it?' and then clear off, having bought nothing. Miserable creatures!

A few minutes later and the barn door creaked. The children tiptoed back in and, once again, took aside the pitchfork, yanked up the hay bale beneath and began filling up the hole below.

'That's the lot. Oh isn't it a relief to get this treasure safely hidden,' whispered Lou, placing the bale back over the top of it. This time, she threw her jacket over the bale to mark what was below. That was a better bet than the pitchfork since they would now be making their beds in the hay for the rest of the night. They wouldn't want to roll on top of it by accident.

'Safe from the clutches of Creepy,' she added.

'I still can't believe how that man got on our trail,' said Jack, 'but at least we've finally outwitted him. Wouldn't it have been sickening if we'd taken it back to the campsite only for him to steal it from us in the dead of night?'

'Yes and my guess is that is exactly what he will try to do tonight,' said Lou, sitting on a bale. 'Neither it nor us would have been safe in our beds.'

'Oh what a horrible thought,' said Emily, with a shiver. 'At least we're perfectly safe in here. Tomorrow we will have to share the good news with your parents, Becky. They'll be astounded!'

'They will also be rich,' said Lou, 'and rightly so. This treasure belongs first and foremost to them since it was found on their land and let's be honest they need the money.'

'Yes,' said Becky, 'or we wouldn't be able to live here for much longer. Dad loves farming, it's his passion but it doesn't bring in enough money. Oh it will mean the world to us to be able to stay here.'

Lou looked at her in the torchlight and nodded understandingly. Lou did understand of course – her parents had nearly lost their holiday home at Abersoch for the same reason.

'Lou, I'm really sorry for my behaviour earlier in the week. I don't know why I acted that way,' continued Becky.

'Nor do I,' replied Lou. 'But it's sorted now. We couldn't have seen off Mr Creepy without you today. You can be proud of what you've done, we all can. There'll be plenty of time to talk it through in the morning. For now, let's get some sleep. If we snuggle up together we should be reasonably warm.'

Dr Malcolm Finchfield listened in disgust. How dare they call him insulting names like "Mr Creepy". He had a good mind to find that pitchfork and give them a jolly sharp prod with it. Worse than that, they were planning to sleep in the barn, right on top of the treasure!

This was an unexpected and most unwelcome development, particularly as the farmer's daughter was clearly now in league with them. Aah, had she been deliberately delaying him earlier from going into the tunnels with her easy charm and friendly banter?

Drat her, the others hadn't been to Lichfield at all that day – they'd been too busy lining their pockets. She'd lied to him. He would do his best to make sure her parents didn't get a penny from that treasure. He'd say he found it somewhere else, so they'd have no claim to it.

What was he to do now? There was nothing for it but to slip out of the barn, call Duncan to come straightaway and then the pair of them would have to start shipping out as the kids slept. If they woke up, they would have to be bound and gagged until they were done. Drat and blast, Creepy could have done without this sort of palaver in the middle of the night.

He made himself wait half an hour or so until he could tell by their heavy breathing and the occasional sigh and snore they were asleep. With any luck, after their exciting day, they would sleep soundly.

Creepy extricated himself from the hay bales, stepped onto the barn floor as quietly as he could and tiptoed round the haystack in the dark. He knew from memory where the door was and anyway, faint chinks of moonlight could be seen through holes in the wood. He would have to take care to nudge it open without too much of a creak.

The important thing was to get Duncan along quickly and then, with any luck, the pair of them might be able to haul everything away without the children waking up.

Crash! Mr Creepy tripped over the pitchfork which Lou had allowed to slither to the stone floor. He fell with an almighty clatter and yelped as the prongs embedded themselves painfully into his legs.

Lou, who had gone to sleep with her torch next to her, awoke instantly and snapped it on with lightning speed. She directed its beam straight towards the sound. There, blinking in the bright light, was none other than Mr Creepy, slowly extracting himself from the pitchfork's grip.

CHAPTER EIGHTEEN

Disaster strikes

FOR a moment, Creepy looked crestfallen and dishevelled, but he soon regained his composure.

'Quick everyone, wake up,' shouted Lou. She kept her torch trained on Creepy and tried hard to sound calm although she didn't feel it. 'What on earth are you doing in here, following us about and spying on us in the middle of the night? How dare you! Get out of here NOW!

'Or you'll do what, my dear?' replied Creepy. 'Surely I have as much right to be in this barn as you do. I might ask you the same question, what are you doing here at this hour?'

Creepy flicked the switch for the single electric bulb which hung from the rafters of the barn roof and stood in front of the door, lest any of them try and make a run for it.

'We are here having a sleep-over in this barn with my parents' full permission,' said Becky, not strictly truthfully. 'You have no right to be here and I'd advise you to leave before I call my parents.'

She pulled her mobile phone from her pocket and flicked it open. Lou winced. That was not a good idea. Before Becky's finger had a chance to start tapping on the display, Creepy lunged across, snatched it from her and zipped it into his coat pocket.

He gave one of his thin-lipped, greasy smiles. 'I'll have everyone else's mobile phones if I may. Hand them over now, or I will go through your pockets.'

'Aah Lou isn't it?' said Creepy to Lou, who shuddered at his use of her name. 'You're the feisty one I believe. Hand over your mobile phone please.'

'I'll do no such thing,' retorted Lou.

While Creepy's attention was on Lou, Jack saw an opportunity. He slowly pulled his own mobile from his pocket. He had the number for the farm stored on it. He tapped a couple of buttons but to his dismay he saw that the display remained dark. The phone was off! He had switched it off earlier not wanting it to ring out when they were trying to move about silently.

Jack switched it on, pushing it under a hay bale as he did so, to muffle the welcome tune it played as it came to life. He stiffened as the jingle rang out and looked at Creepy. Amazingly, Creepy didn't hear it – maybe his hearing was not as good as it once was – but he did notice Jack fidgeting.

'What are you up to, boy?' he said.

'Aah, I think I can guess. Hand the phone over now boy, or I will take it from you and smash it to pieces on the stone floor,' said Creepy, his well-heeled, educated voice suddenly sounding harsh and cruel.

Jack had no choice but to do as he said, but he made a meal out of it, hoping to provide a distraction to help Lou. He held the phone out to Creepy but then snatched it back as the man tried to take it. Creepy grappled with him and pulled it from Jack's hand.

Lou, seizing the moment, pulled her mobile phone from the coat she'd taken off and ran towards the door. Creepy hadn't the time to turn round but he put out one of his long legs and tripped her. She fell to the ground bruising her forehead. Her mobile skittered across the barn floor. Creepy grabbed her and threw her down into the hay.

To the horror of the children he reached into his pocket and pulled out a penknife and opened up the blade. Creepy had no intention of hurting anyone with it, he was far too refined for such behaviour, but they didn't know that of course.

Their shock bought him a few useful seconds. He

pulled up the twine from one of the bales and cut a length off. He grabbed Lou's wrists, wrapped the twine around and bound them tight. Then it was Jack's turn and then David's. They were now too scared to put up any resistance.

'Now listen,' said Lou, 'you leave the girls alone, don't you dare tie them up.'

'No need,' said Creepy, his smooth voice returning as he relaxed a bit. 'They're no threat. As for you pair, I'll need your phones as well,' he said to David and Emily.

'They are 11 and 10 years old for goodness' sake,' snarled Lou. 'They don't have a mobile phone.'

'Good for them,' said Creepy, smiling unpleasantly. 'Now all we need to do is to phone a friend – I think that's what they say on that TV quiz show isn't it?'

Creepy snickered at his painfully weak joke as the others looked on in dismay and disgust. He reached into his pocket for his phone.

'If my battery's gone flat, I'll use one of yours if that's ok,' joked Creepy.

'Hang on,' said Lou, desperately trying to think of anything she could to distract him. 'I don't understand, what is your game? Why are you doing this – what is the point of tying us up when we're just kids camping out in a barn for the fun of it?'

'My dear we all know perfectly well why we're here – we're all looking for the missing Anglo-Saxon treasure, isn't that right?' replied Creepy, matter of factly. 'Now this is something of huge historical importance to the nation. It cannot be allowed to fall into the hands of mere children. An antiquities expert such as myself can take proper care of it and ensure that it is handed over to the relevant authorities.'

'You're a liar,' retorted Lou, her eyes blazing. 'A sneaking, creepy liar. We know you are using a false name, your name isn't Andrew Fitzgerald at all, it's

Malcolm something or other, unless that is a fake name too. We don't have the treasure so if you want it, I suggest you let us go and get on with the job of looking for it.'

Creepy was shaken by her use of his real Christian name. How on earth did she know that? He had to get moving quickly. This could become dangerous.

'I would suggest it is you who is lying, young lady,' he replied, icily. 'You know perfectly well where the treasure is and if you are inviting me to go and look for it I will happily do so. How about we start by lifting the hay bale you threw your jacket over and see what's underneath?

With a dramatic flourish, Creepy pulled the bale up and there, of course, carefully piled and sprinkled with loose straw, was the entire contents of the priceless hoard.

The children gasped. He knew where the treasure was and he was going to take it away from under their noses as soon as he'd called his accomplice to come with the getaway car. They couldn't stop him!

'Now, if you'll excuse me, I have a phone call to make,' said Creepy, tapping numbers into his mobile phone.

The children had no choice but to listen helplessly as he gave directions to his accomplice who was, apparently, only 15 minutes away. Creepy explained about the children and to their relief, they heard him say they would be let go once the van was loaded up. But the treasure would be whisked away which they had put so much effort into finding! Treasure which would have secured the otherwise uncertain future of the Owens' family farm. Treasure which ought to be shared by the whole nation – not sold off to wealthy private collectors to make the likes of Creepy rich. It was sickening beyond words.

'Aah,' said Creepy to his mate. 'Oh goodness, you're right, wouldn't do to leave that. While you're on your way I'll nip back to the field and grab my camping gear.

It won't take more than 10 minutes.'

Pity, thought Lou, the absent-minded fool had forgotten about his tent and belongings. That would have proved a means of tracking him down. Even if they did, she thought despairingly, Creepy would bluff his way through and claim it was he who found the treasure. He would deny keeping them prisoner, of course. There would be no proof. If he got away with the treasure that was it, it would be gone for good and what could possibly be done to stop him? Nothing!

How on earth had he managed to work out that they were moving the hoard to the barn? He must have been watching out for them yet they had been so careful, surely they had? Then she remembered with a groan, the flicker of torchlight which Creepy might have seen if he was on the prowl. Oh and the geese – they had quacked like mad things. The noise had probably alerted him even if the torchlight hadn't.

Noise! That was a thought. Perhaps they could shout the place down and get help that way. Best to wait for Creepy to clear off first.

'Right,' said Creepy, giving them another greasy smile. 'I'm going to head back to the campsite to pick up my things and my erm, colleague will be along shortly to help move the hoard to a safe location. You will then be released.'

'When you are gone, Mr Creepy, we will shout our heads off,' yelled Becky at him, who had been thinking along the same lines as Lou. 'We'll make such a racket it will wake the dead!'

'Will it?' said Creepy. 'Well that will never do, that would be most unfortunate. They might start ambling around and haunting us. Thank you for sharing that information with me. It should have occurred to me that you might do that but I'm not at my best at 1.30 in the morning, you know.'

He grabbed a handful of hay, seized Becky and pushed it into her mouth. 'Get off me you creepy swine,' she mumbled as he pulled a length of twine around her mouth and fastened it tight.

'Help, help!' yelled the others as Creepy then gagged first Lou then Jack in the same way. With their hands tied behind their backs they had no chance of stopping him. Creepy even gagged poor Emily.

'Oh and one more thing,' he said, looking at Becky and Emily, 'seeing as I've kindly let you keep your hands free, I better secure this treasure in case you try to move some of it, hoping I won't notice.'

Creepy got his penknife out again and cut some longish lengths. He placed a hay bale firmly back over the hoard and pulled the twine hard over the top. He then made it fast to the adjoining bales. It was now impossible to lift off.

With that, Creepy pushed open the barn door, taking care not to make it creak, and closed it behind him gently.

Then the children heard the sickening sound of the bolts being slid shut. He had locked them in. They were prisoners!

CHAPTER NINETEEN

Becky makes amends

LOU cursed, but it came out as an unintelligible gurgle. They had been well and truly defeated. Bound, gagged and locked in with not one but two men poised to cart off treasure which they had absolutely no right to.

In the end, Becky, who had been so helpful earlier that day, had let them down that evening. Her silly mistakes, in particular, needing torchlight to find a barn on the farm where she had lived all her life were simply appalling. Then alerting Creepy to the fact that they had mobile phones on them – unforgivable. She'd even warned him they would shout the place down, hence his decision to gag them.

Yet I've been no star of the show either, thought Lou to herself, bitterly.

Lou looked around the barn, desperately trying to think of something they could do. With her mouth full of hay and her wrists tied, there weren't many options. Was there anything sharp she could use to cut the twine? She pulled herself up as best she could from the haystack onto the stone floor. Becky and Emily, whose hands Creepy hadn't bothered to tie, tried their best to undo the twine around the others' wrists and mouths. Creepy had tied the knots far too tight, of course.

Desperate to atone for her earlier blunders, Becky looked around the barn with Lou trying to think of something which might work. Already a couple of minutes had passed. She had one big advantage – the use of her hands. What could she do with them? Not much, it would appear.

Lou was trying to attract her attention. She nudged her shoulder and thrust her wrists out in the direction of the barn wall. She was nodding towards the wall. Becky looked in that direction and didn't know what she meant at first. Oh yes, a couple of keys were hanging up.

Lou clearly thought they might be of use to open the barn door. They wouldn't be, of course. The door was bolted from the outside. Lou knew that but hoped that the keys might open another exit somewhere.

Unfortunately there was only a single door – the one they were locked behind. The keys were no use at all, they were for the tractor.

Becky glanced over at the tractor, sitting at the back of the barn. It was a handsome, bright green machine. She stared at it for a minute or so as if in a trance. Lou looked at her impatiently. What *was* Becky playing at? Were the keys any use to them or not?

Becky had noticed something significant about the tractor. It still had its front loader attached – a big metal bucket with huge hydraulic arms used to move bales of hay or crops from one place to another. Her dad was currently gathering in the harvest so he had left it on.

She tried to tell the others now standing on the stone floor in front of the haystack to move aside. With a gag over her mouth, they couldn't understand her. She pulled the keys off the hook and made a pushing movement with her hands. She rattled the keys and pointed towards the tractor.

Jack, David and Emily had no idea what Becky was trying to say but Lou guessed and she shooed the others backwards onto the haystack. They had to keep well out of the way of this. Lou gave Becky's shoulder a rub and nodded to her to indicate her approval. It was a bold and courageous plan and it was their only hope.

They watched as Becky ran to the other end of the barn, climbed up to the tractor's cab and tried first one key then the other in the door. The second one worked, so the other must be to start it up. Becky got inside, pushed the key into the ignition and turned it.

The engine started first time, with a low-pitched throaty chug. She switched on the headlights, relieved that she had remembered which button to press. She had to be quick, exhaust fumes would be dangerous in an enclosed space.

The space they were in wasn't going to stay enclosed for long, however. Becky might not be a typical farm girl, with her love of make-up and disdain for farmyard chores, but in her 14 years she'd learnt a thing or two, including how to drive her dad's tractor. In truth, it was one of the few things she had enjoyed, riding it up and down the fields with a plough attached to the back or a seed dispenser or even a muck spreader, although that could be a bit pongy.

Those skills would stand her in good stead now. She engaged first gear, brought up the clutch and drove the tractor gently out onto the stone floor. It was now a straight run towards the barn door. She had two feet of space behind her, so she put the tractor into reverse until it was backed up against the rear wall.

Then she tapped the joystick to bring the front loader downwards from near vertical. The huge metal bucket with jagged teeth now extended straight out ahead of the tractor as if attached to a pair of long, outstretched arms.

She checked carefully that the others were well clear. They were – Lou had got them out of the way. Becky put the tractor back into first gear so that it was ready to be propelled forwards. She counted from one to three and took a deep breath.

Then, as if piloting a plane cleared for take-off, she drove the tractor with its outstretched digger bucket as fast as she could towards the barn door.

As it loomed in front of her she gripped the steering

wheel tightly and kept her foot down hard on the accelerator pedal. Right at the last second, she shut her eyes.

Crash! It was like a bomb going off. The wooden door splintered into pieces and burst free from its hinges.

For a moment, silence. Then the startled geese, furious at being awakened yet again, began to quack their heads off and so did the ducks. The pigs grunted and oinked, the coos mooed and even the sheep in the fields awoke and start baaing. Creepy, half way across the field by now, stopped in his tracks and turned round. He stared back at the farmyard, uncomprehending.

The barn door, which for several years had been struggling to stay upright, lay in bits on the ground. The children were no longer prisoners! Lou, Jack, David and Emily could now walk straight through a wide open space. Lou gestured with her hand not to approach the tractor. Becky was high up in the cab and might not easily see them. Those huge wheels were dangerous.

She had not finished her mission. The tractor delivered the final insult to the shattered barn door by rolling straight over it. Then it was off through the farmyard and out into the field. Becky guessed Creepy would be about half way up it and sped quickly through the gate in pursuit.

To the man's great discomfort, two bright, closely-set headlamps began to head straight at him. He stood, rooted to the spot, not knowing whether to run or in which direction. To his relief, the headlamps veered off towards the end of the field. Thank goodness, thought Creepy, the farmer must be doing some night-time work with his tractor. You had to hand it to these farmers – up at all hours, working every spare minute.

Creepy resumed his walk towards his tent. He had to gather his things quickly. He had no idea what had caused that terrific noise but he didn't understand the countryside and thought perhaps some logical reason existed for it.

His relief did not last for long. The tractor's headlights appeared again, this time pointing down the field. It was directly in his path. Whatever was that Mr Owen up to? Not wishing to run, lest it appear suspicious, Creepy began to stroll towards the side of the field.

The tractor began driving towards the side of the field, too! To his horror, he could see in the headlights that its enormous front loader was attached. Its great ugly looking digger bucket had been lowered almost to the ground, as if poised to scoop something up.

Creepy, still determined to think that this was some strange agricultural exercise for which there was a perfectly rational explanation, sought to resume his walk towards the end of the field and back to his tent.

The tractor circled around him again and this time headed straight for him. He froze in terror, then turned around and began to run, like he had never run before, towards the farmhouse. He didn't know what was going on, but he didn't like it.

The tractor followed right behind him. Creepy tried to run in a zigzag, so the tractor began to zigzag and then, terrifyingly, it began papping its horn loudly and flashing its lights on and off. There was no doubt about it, the tractor was after him. Some madman must have got hold of it, and was seeking to capture him in that huge metal bucket!

Becky guessed Creepy would now seek to run into the farmyard and escape via the lane if he could. She could not follow him along a public road and it would be difficult to head him off. Sure enough, he began to run towards the main gate. It was shut and to her delight, their sheepdog Flash was standing in front of it, barking loudly.

Creepy skidded to a halt, not wishing to pick a fight with that bad-tempered dog. He doubled back and in desperation started to run in a circle round the farmyard. Becky went as close to him as she dared and, at just the right moment, put the full beam lights on – illuminating a tempting wooden fence ahead.

Creepy saw it and ran towards it gratefully, pulling himself over and out of reach of the demented tractor. He jumped down into what he hoped was a pleasant green field the other side. His boots gave the most awful squelch. Creepy couldn't understand why it was so boggy. Then came an indignant 'oink!'.

The fence wasn't bordering a field at all as Becky knew perfectly well – he had climbed into the pigsty! There was an enormous mummy pig inside with a squealing litter of piglets. Seeking to protect her youngsters, the huge creature lunged at Creepy and butted him with her snout. He stepped backwards and fell over one of the piglets, landing face down in a great pile of mud and muck.

Meanwhile, the geese, still furious at the interruptions to their sleep that night, waddled over and began hissing, looking for someone to peck. Becky gave a long toot on the horn and flashed her lights on and off. Mr Owen's livestock struck up a discordant racket. It was like the worst orchestra imaginable.

~~~~~

Mr and Mrs Owen always slept soundly after long, busy days in the fresh air and the walls of their farmhouse were thick. But not even they could snooze through an exploding barn door and the ensuing commotion. They got up, put their dressing gowns on and looked through their window.

To their astonishment, they saw the lights of their tractor zigzagging across the field, flashing on and off and the horn blaring. They assumed youths must have broken in and were busy joy-riding in it.

Mr Owen telephoned the police immediately. Then they heard banging on the back door! Mrs Owen opened the
~~~~~

window and shouted, 'who's there?'

It was Lou, Jack, David and Emily but they couldn't speak of course. They were still gagged. They went round and stood beneath the couple's window. Under the weak light of the moon, Mr and Mrs Owen could just about make out the group of children standing there, mouths stuffed with hay and bound with twine and all, save Emily, with their wrists tied!

'Oh my goodness,' exclaimed Mrs Owen. 'It's the children who are camping in the field! Look at them!'

The couple tore downstairs and brought them inside. Mrs Owen got a knife and cut them free.

'You need to come quickly,' said Lou. 'Becky's in the tractor and she's rounding up the man you know as Mr Fitzgerald – the one who's camping in our field in the red tent. He tied us up and imprisoned us in the barn. I can't explain everything now but you need to call the police and have him arrested.'

'I've called them already, they're on the way,' said Mr Owen.

'Come on,' said Lou, before Becky's dad had a chance to ask any more questions. They raced into the farmyard where Becky, her mouth still gagged, was sitting in the tractor with the digger bucket raised and blocking Creepy's attempts to climb back out of the pigsty.

Suddenly he ran to the other side and tried to vault over the top. Becky expertly swung the tractor round that side and blocked him with the digger bucket.

In her rear view mirror, she saw headlights and a blue light flashing on and off. The police! They had arrived!

Mr Owen swung back the gate to let them in. Becky switched the engine off and alighted from the tractor cab. She still had her gag on, and her mum quickly cut it off.

Mr Owen looked from one child to another in the most utter bafflement.

'Will someone please tell me what the devil is going

on?' he demanded.

'The devil is in that pigsty,' replied Becky, pointing dramatically at Creepy who was blinking nervously in the light, his face black with pig muck.

CHAPTER TWENTY

The devil in the pigsty

IN truth, Creepy did look something like a devil – covered in filth from top to toe with the flashing blue strobe lights of the police car making his pale eyes and grey teeth gleam weirdly on and off. He pulled some horrible grimaces as trickles of brown slime dripped from his moustache and onto his lips.

Flash the sheepdog, aware that he was some kind of intruder, was now sitting right underneath him, eager for another glimpse of Creepy's tempting white shins.

'There's been a mistake, a dreadful misunderstanding,' spluttered Creepy.

'He need locking up, he's a danger to . . .' began Becky, the drama of it rather overwhelming her.

'Becky let me speak,' said Lou. 'Officer this man, who calls himself Andrew Fitzgerald but whose real name we believe is Malcolm something, held us prisoner in the barn. He gagged us and bound our wrists before locking the barn door from the outside. He phoned for an accomplice to come and meet him at the farm and their intention was to drive away with a priceless hoard of Anglo-Saxon treasure.

'We, the five of us,' she said, pointing to Jack, David, Emily and Becky, 'found the treasure in an underground cave beneath Mr and Mrs Owen's land. We were searching for the hoard with their permission and their daughter helped us to find it. We moved it to the barn for safekeeping because we feared this man would attempt to seize it from us. He has been looking for it on their land without permission and I believe he had every intention of taking it away.

'The hoard needs to be handed to the authorities and the British Museum informed. It's of great historical value and we are the legitimate finders of it and Mr and Mrs Owen are the landowners with a rightful claim to it.

'In trying to steal it, this man spied on us, ransacked our tents, stole property from us and then tonight, as I've said, bound and gagged us and took us prisoner.'

Mr and Mrs Owen and the police officers listened to Lou's account in amazement.

'Erm no,' interjected Creepy. 'That's not how it happened at all. I am a respected antiques dealer and authority on Anglo-Saxon treasure and the recently-discovered Staffordshire Hoard. I have long been aware of the possibility of there being a second hoard and the youngsters' own mother, Liz Johnson, kindly sent me a copy of an old Victorian book which led me here in search of it. She told me that the children had gone over to look for it and I thought I would come along and lend my assistance.'

'So that's what brought you here,' cried David in astonishment. 'Our own mother told you!'

'David, she would have done so innocently, not realising that this fraudster who uses fake names would come and try to take it from us,' Lou reassured him.

'Will you please climb out of that pigsty and give your name sir,' said the police officer politely to Creepy.

'It is Doctor Malcolm Finchfield,' replied Creepy in as dignified a voice as he could muster, after he had hauled his bruised body back over the fence.

'Louise is right, that's not the name he gave us when he rang up asking to stay here,' said Mrs Owen. 'He spoke to my daughter Becky and booked in as Mr Andrew Fitzgerald.'

'Is it true that you made these children prisoners in the barn?' said the officer.

'Absolutely not, that's preposterous,' he replied.

'Then ask him to explain why he has three mobile phones belonging to me, Jack and Becky zipped up in his coat pocket,' said Lou.

'Will you empty your pockets please, Dr Finchfield,' said the officer.

'I have never been so humiliated in my life,' said Creepy. 'These are all my phones,' he said, fetching them out one by one. 'I keep spares in case the batteries run out.'

'Really sir, including this rather girlish-looking pink one?' said the officer, disbelievingly.

Turning to the children, the officer said, 'tell me, how did you escape from the barn?'

'I'm sorry, dad,' said Becky, turning to her father. 'I'm afraid you'll need a new barn door.' She faltered, fearing he would be furious, so Lou told him exactly how it ended up being smashed to pieces.

'You'll find the entire contents of the hoard under a couple of hay bales,' continued Lou. 'It's from an underground cave in the sandstone ridge on your land. It must be worth a fortune and should bring you in enough money to keep you farming here for a long time. We know it's a struggle for you at the moment.'

'It is,' said Mr Owen, 'that's one reason why that barn door was so rickety, in fact most of them are. The barns are falling apart because we've not had the money to maintain them. Well I don't know what to say, I'm astonished and proud of you all,' he said, giving his daughter a rare hug.

'When I drove out of the barn, dad,' said Becky, recovering her composure, 'I realised that Creepy would be halfway back to his tent – he was going to get his camping things so his mate could whisk him off with the treasure. So I went after him in the tractor, blocked his path and chased him back to the farmyard. He then panicked and climbed over the fence into the pigsty.'

'You were coming at me like a lunatic,' growled Creepy, 'and I'll remind you that my name is Dr Finchfield, not Creepy.'

'Right,' said the officer. 'I've heard enough. Dr Finchfield, or whatever your name is, I'm arresting you on suspicion of attempted theft, assault and illegal imprisonment. Come this way please.'

'Hang on,' said the other officer, 'this is a brand new patrol car. We can't have him getting in covered in pig muck, the inspector will go mad. The station only took delivery of it last week. We'll have to send one of the old vans to pick him up.'

The children looked at each other and then at Creepy and laughed. He grimaced horribly and said, 'drat you all.'

Mr and Mrs Owen and the children left the police and their new prisoner in the farmyard to sort that little matter out. They all needed a good strong mug of tea.

'Come on everyone, let's get you into the farmhouse kitchen and get the kettle on,' said Mrs Owen. 'We'll have some toast or something, I don't think any of us will sleep another wink for the rest of the night.'

'Hey you youngsters,' the arresting officer called after them. 'Nice work! We'll take some statements off you in the morning and you make sure you get everything reported properly to the British Museum. If the hoard is declared to be treasure then you'll be in for a huge reward as finders and so will you and your wife, Mr Owen, as the landowners. It will be like the Staffordshire Hoard all over again.'

'Marvellous, I suppose we couldn't have a peek at that treasure tonight could we?' said Mr Owen.

'Certainly not,' replied his wife. 'It can wait until the morning. Now into the kitchen with you.'

The children looked at each other and smiled.

'Well done David,' said Jack to his younger brother,

ruffling his hair. 'I might have known your theory of the missing treasure was so crazy it would actually come true.'

'What about the theory that we weren't supposed to come across any baddies and end up getting taken prisoner this time,' said Emily, with something of a twinkle in her eye.

'Look, so long as you've got a farm girl with a tractor to smash her way out of a tight spot and round up the baddies, you're ok,' joked Lou.

'You are a mad thing though,' she added, turning towards Becky with an admiring grin, as they walked towards the farmhouse. 'I'm not sure even I would have dared to do that. You know, I took you for a stuck-up, indoors girl who knew nothing about farming, but the way you handled that tractor was amazing. I'll have to get you to teach me!'

'Well,' said Becky, 'I don't know why but I've always loved driving the tractor. That's the one thing on the farm that I've always been happy doing. I knew that door was rotting and waiting to fall off its hinges. My mum's been telling my dad to replace it for ages.'

'He'll soon have the money to,' said Lou. 'It will be enough to keep this farm in your family for another 200 years I should think. It was down to your bravery today. It wouldn't have happened without you.'

'I'm so glad Lou,' said Becky, tears of relief and happiness in her eyes. 'I wanted to make up for what I'd done.'

'Tell me something,' said Lou, 'why were you so mean to us, especially to me? I could never work that out. Was it because you really thought we'd spirit away the treasure? We didn't even expect to find any.'

'No, it wasn't so much that. I was jealous I suppose,' admitted Becky, 'that you were all younger than me but far more self-assured and you were on holiday without your parents, which I've never done. Anyway I'm not always very nice to people and it's true, I am stuck up and vain at times.'

'It's because you're an only child like me and you get lonely and bored,' said Lou. 'You're a good person underneath and I hoped you would be. Stay as you are now and you'll have loads of friends, including us.'

'Hey Lou,' said Becky, pulling her back, 'all that treasure – you and the others will share it won't you? My parents will want you to and so do I.'

'I don't know,' said Lou, grinning. 'I don't need to be rich, not in money anyway and nor do the others. The fun for us was finding it. But I could do with that cup of tea!'

LOU ELLIOTT MYSTERY ADVENTURES:

1. Smugglers at Whistling Sands
2. The Missing Treasure
3. Something Strange in the Cellar
4. Trouble at Chumley Towers

George Chedzoy works from home as a novelist and freelance writer. He lives in North Wales with his wife and two young children. He's always pleased to hear from readers and you can contact him directly on email or Twitter (see below). All books in this series can be ordered from bookshops or from Amazon.

George's blog is at http://georgechedzoy.blogspot.com
Twitter: @georgechedzoy
Email: georgechedzoy@hotmail.co.uk

21795285R00111

Printed in Great Britain
by Amazon